"Did you want to come in? I'll make you hot chocolate this time," Amy asked.

"No, I just wanted to see you were safe," Heath replied.

"So you could leave?"

"Something like that."

Amy wished she could be angry with him, but it wasn't that easy. How could she be angry with someone that wonderful? He spoke so well and knew how to make hollandaise sauce without checking a recipe and stood tall when danger called. Not the usual wanderer looking for a job. And that left the question "Why?" She instinctively knew it was a question that would only make him turn away.

Some things were left in the past where they belonged. Everyone deserved at least one free pass, one "do over." Maybe that's the way it was for Heath....

JILLIAN HART

makes her home in Washington State, where she has lived most of her life. When Jillian is not hard at work on her next story, she loves to read, go to lunch with her friends and spend quiet evenings with her family.

SWEET
BLESSINGS

JILLIAN HART

Steeple
Hill®

Published by Steeple Hill Books™

STEEPLE HILL BOOKS

Steeple
Hill®

ISBN 0-373-81209-4

SWEET BLESSINGS

Copyright © 2005 by Jill Strickler

www.SteepleHill.com

Printed in U.S.A.

Every good and perfect gift is from above, coming down from the Father of the heavenly lights, who does not change like shifting shadows.

—*James* 1:17

Chapter One

The jingle of the bell above the door announced a late customer to the diner.

Amy McKaslin glanced at the clock above the cash register that said it was eight minutes to ten, which was closing time, and sized up the man standing like a shadow just inside the glass doorway.

He wasn't someone local or anyone she recognized. He was tall with a build to match. He wore nothing more than a flannel shirt unbuttoned and untucked over a T-shirt and wash-worn jeans. He had that frazzled, numb look of a man who'd been traveling hard and long without enough rest or food.

Road exhaustion. She'd seen it lots of times. He wasn't the first driver who'd taken this exit off the interstate. It happened all the time. With any luck, he'd be a quick in-and-out, looking for nothing more than a shot of caffeine and a bite before he got back on the road.

That was a much better prospect than last night, when a half dozen high-school kids had piled into a booth. Amy enjoyed the teenage crowd, but it had been nearly midnight before she could lock up and head home. Not good when her son was waiting for her, and she was paying a baby-sitter by the hour.

Tonight, Westin would be waiting, too, and on a school night when little boys should be fast asleep. He was an anxious one, always worrying, and she prayed the lone stranger had somewhere he had to go, too. Someone who was waiting for him. She turned the sign in the window to closed before any teenage clique decided to wander in.

Forcing a smile after being on her feet since 6:00 a.m., she grabbed a laminated menu. "Table or booth?"

The loner shrugged, looking past her as if he didn't see her at all. His eyes had that un-focused look drivers got when they'd been staring down pavement and white lines for too long, and the purple smudges beneath spoke of his exhaustion.

Yep, me too, buddy. She led him past the row of tables, washed and prepped for morning, to the booths in the corner, where the night windows reflected the brightly lit dining area back at her. Already she was thinking of home. Of her little boy's after-supper call.

"Come home, Mommy," he'd said in that quiet way he had. "I told Kelly not to read me any more of my story. You were gonna tonight, remember?"

She remembered. Nothing was more serious than the promises she made to her little boy. Almost there, she thought, as she watched the clock's hands creep another minute closer to ten. Aware of the man behind her making less noise than a shadow, she slid the menu onto the corner booth.

She whipped out her pad. "What can I get you to drink?"

Haggard. That was one word to describe him. The overhead light glared harshly on his sun-browned skin and whisker-stubbled jaw as he folded his over-six-foot frame behind the table. "Coffee."

"Leaded or decaf?"

"I want the real thing. Don't bother to make fresh. If you got something that's been sitting awhile, I'd rather have it." He pushed the menu back at her. "A burger, too. With bacon if it's not too much trouble."

"Sure thing." As she scribbled up the ticket, already walking away, something drew her to look one more time.

He had gone to staring sightlessly out the window, appearing tired and haunted. The black night reflected back the illusion of the well-lit café and his hollow face. The man wasn't able to see through the windows to the world outside. It was within that he was looking.

Her heart twisted in recognition. There was something about him that was familiar. Not the look of him, since she'd never met him before, but it was that faraway glint in his eyes. One that she recognized by feel.

She, too, knew what it was like to feel haunted by the past. Life made a mark on everyone. She didn't know how she saw this in this stranger, but she was certain she wasn't wrong. The regrets and despair of the past yanked within her, like a summer trout caught on a fishing hook. As she grabbed the carafe from the burner, where it had been sitting since the end of the supper rush, she risked another glance at the man.

He sat motionless with his elbows braced on the table's edge and his face resting in his hands.

Hopelessness. Yeah, she knew how that felt, too. Pain rose up in her chest, pointed like an arrow's tip, and she didn't know if it was the stranger she felt sympathy for or the girl she used to be. Maybe both.

She slid the cup and saucer onto the table. "I hope this is strong enough. If not, I'll be happy to make a fresh pot that will hold up a spoon. You just ask."

"Thank you, ma'am." He didn't make eye contact as he reached for the sugar dispenser on the small lazy Susan in the middle of the table.

Whatever troubled him on this cool late-spring night, she hoped at least a cup of coffee and a meal would strengthen him.

Something sad might have happened to him to make him a traveler tonight, she speculated. Maybe some family tragedy that had torn him from his normal life and had him driving on lonely roads through the night-time. She knew that pain, too, and closed her mind against it. Some pain never healed. Some losses ran deep as the soul.

She put in the order, catching sight of her sister. "This is the last one. I already turned the sign over."

Rachel glanced at the ticket and pivoted on her heels to remove one last beef patty from the cooler. "If you want to take the floors, I'll total out the till. Have those other guys left yet?"

"No." Amy had almost refused them service when they came in, a little too bright-eyed and loud. They'd quieted down once they started eating. "They were just finishing up when I walked by."

"Good. I don't like them. I know they've been in before, but not this late."

Amy knew what her sister didn't say. Not when we're alone with them. Yeah, that had occurred to her, too. Big-city crime didn't happen in their little Montana town, but that didn't mean a woman ought to let down her guard.

She could see the two rough-looking men through the kitchen door with their heads bent as they both studied the totaled check.

"Don't worry," she reassured her sister. "We aren't exactly alone with them."

"Good." Rachel slapped the meat on the grill. "We may get out of here before eleven, if we're lucky. Say, how's Westin holding up?"

Westin. Amy's stomach clenched thinking of all her little one had gone through. "He had a rough day, and now we're just waiting for the test results. They can do a lot for asthma nowadays. It won't be like what Ben went through."

They both fell silent for a moment, remembering how ill their brother had been when he was Westin's age. They'd had to keep oxygen in the house just in case of a severe attack. They'd almost lost him a few times, calling the ambulance while his lips turned blue and he struggled for breath that was impossible for him to draw in.

Amy's stomach clamped into a hard, worried ball. It wouldn't be like that for Westin. She would make sure of it. How, she didn't know, but she certainly had the strength to will it. That, with prayers, had to make a difference, right?

"I slipped a little gift for him into your coat

pocket. Don't get mad at me. I couldn't resist."

"You got him that video game, didn't you? You're spoiling him, you know. It was supposed to wait until his report card."

"Yeah, yeah, but you know me." Sweetheart that she was, with a heart-shaped face and all gentleness, Rachel shrugged helplessly, as if she had no choice but to spoil her nephew.

Since it was impossible to be even a little mad at Rachel, Amy just rolled her eyes. "I'm sure he'll be thrilled."

"Oh, excellent!" Pleased, Rachel set the hamburger buns on to toast.

Yep, it was hard to do anything but be deeply grateful for her big sister. Amy gave thanks, as she always did. They'd lost their parents long ago, when they were all still kids. It had only made her hold tight to the loved ones in her life now. Her sisters, her brother, and her son. So tight, there was no way she'd let them go.

It looked as if the two men, who'd initially been upset there was no alcohol served in the diner, were getting ready to leave. Although Amy couldn't smell alcohol on them, she suspected they'd imbibed sometime earlier in the evening. Not that she approved, but there was no outward reason to refuse service. In a small town, turning away customers tended to be bad for business.

Still, they'd done nothing more than laugh a little too loudly while they'd waited for their burgers. Now, with any luck, they'd pay and be on their way. She'd breathe easier once the door was safely shut behind them. They had that rowdy look to them. Men like that…no, it was best not to remember.

Her life was different now. *She* was different.

There was a ruckus from table five. "Hey, waitress! What pie do you got?"

Oh no, and here she'd been wishing them out the door. Amy had to dig deep to remain patient and courteous. She didn't like the way they were looking at her. As if she were a slice of pie with whipped cream on top. "We have a few slices of apple left."

"Nah. I was hopin' for something sweeter." The one on the left—with a gold cap on one front tooth—gave her a wink.

As if. "I'll be your cashier if you're ready."

"It's too bad about that pie. You must be just about done here. Maybe you'd like to come out with us?"

"No, I have to get home to my little boy." She waited.

One gave her an oh-I'm-not-interested-now look.

The other didn't so much as blink. "Then maybe you need a night out worse than I thought."

"Sorry. Will this be cash or charge?" Hint, hint. *Let's go, boys. Out of my diner.* She waited, trying to be courteous but firm.

"It'll take us a minute." The one who was not so interested in her reached into his back pocket for his wallet.

Good. Rachel's call bell jangled, signaling the last customer's burger was ready. She left the men to their arithmetic, glad for an excuse to put as much distance between them as possible.

She caught a movement in the window's reflection. The loner was in the act of lifting his coffee cup. Had he been watching her?

"Hey, waitress." They were talking to her again.

She dreaded turning around, but these

weren't the first tough customers she'd dealt with. "Yes?"

"Are you sure you don't have a bottle or two hid in back? I know you said you don't got beer to sell. But me and my buddy here sure could use a couple a beers."

"Sorry, we don't have a liquor license."

"What kind of place don't serve beer?"

"A family restaurant." Amy kept her smile in place as she withdrew the order pad from her apron pocket.

The bigger of the two swore.

She flinched. Okay, she didn't want any trouble. She wanted them gone, the faster the better. She pivoted on her heel, hoping this was the end of it. *C'mon, just leave your money and go.*

In the window's reflection, she again noticed the lone stranger. Sitting hunch-shouldered as if uninterested, but his gaze was alert. He didn't move, although she could feel how his every muscle was tensed like a wolf watching his prey. Waiting to spring.

It strengthened her. She knew it was the Lord at work in her life, as He always was. For every bad customer, there was always another who was not.

Thankfully, there was no trouble. The offending parties left a pile of greenbacks and pounded to the door, chewing on toothpicks and making as much noise as possible as they went. The bell chimed when the door shut.

Trouble averted. Relieved, she hurried over to turn the dead bolt. *Thank you, Father.*

Her reflection stared back at her in the glass. She saw a woman of average height and weight, with her hair pulled back in a tight ponytail. Her face was shadowed by too many hollows. The circles beneath her eyes looked like gouges from too many nights without sleep.

Maybe tonight she'd sleep better. A girl had to hope. She had so much to do before she could get home and into her warm bed. There was this one more customer, and then clean-up, and she could be home by eleven, eleven-thirty, depending. Westin would be listening for her. The hard knot in her stomach relaxed a smidgen, just thinking of her little boy. Yeah, she couldn't wait to get home to him. To see his sweet face.

Rachel peered at her over the hand-off counter, where a plate piled high with a deluxe bacon burger and fries waited beneath a warming light. "Our last customer looked road-weary, so I made the burger with an extra patty."

"I thought you might." Amy didn't bother to change the total on the ticket she left on the table with the meal. "Can I get you anything else?"

The lone wolf was staring out the window again. He shook his head.

He seemed so far away. His black hair was cut short, but not too short. Just enough for the cowlick at the crown of his head to stick up. It made him seem vulnerable somehow, this big beefy man with linebacker's shoulders and a presence that could scare off a mountain lion.

Curiosity was going to get the better of her, so before she could get caught staring at him, she left a full ketchup bottle next to the meal ticket and went to collect the money the other men had left.

"I don't believe this. I should have known." She recounted the stack of ones.

"What?" Rachel appeared in the doorway, dishcloth in hand. "Didn't they pay?"

"For only half of the total. I should have watched them closer. I just didn't want to be any nearer to them than I had to be." It wasn't the end of the world. It was only five dollars. "Men like that just make me so mad."

A flash of movement caught her attention. The loner stood with the scrape of his chair. Without a word he took off down the aisle.

She looked at him with surprise.

"Should I give Cameron a call at home?" came the woman's voice from the kitchen doorway. "He can handle it for us."

The waitress dropped the bills back on the table. "It's not worth it. Men like that—"

She didn't finish the statement, but Heath Murdock could read it in her stance. She wrapped her slender arms around her narrow waist as if in comfort and he had to wonder if a man like the two lowlifes that were out in the parking lot had hurt her somewhere down the line. Not just a little, but a lot. And because he knew how that felt, he headed for the door.

The world was a tough place and sometimes it was enough to break a man's soul. There was a lot he couldn't fix that was wrong in this world and in his own life, but this…he could do this. The dead bolt clicked when he turned it and he went outside into the gust of wind that brought new rain with it.

He felt the woman watching him. He didn't know if she approved, or if she was instead one of those ladies who disapproved of any show of strength. But it didn't stop him. He knew what was right. And walking out on a check was stealing, plain and simple. Not to mention the disrespect they'd paid to the perfectly decent waitress who'd done nothing more than remain polite.

A small diner in a small town didn't probably make much in sales. Heath knew he had justice on his side as he stalked across the parking lot. A pickup roared to life. Lights blazed in the blackness, searing his eyes.

Trouble. He could feel it on the knife's edge of the wind. Through the blinding glare of the high beams, he made out a newer-model truck with big dirt-gripping tires. A row of fog lights mounted on the cab were bright enough to spotlight a path to the moon.

The engine roared, as the vehicle vibrated like a predator preparing to attack. Heath didn't have much of a chance of stopping them now. Not when they were already in the cab and behind the wheel. When the engine gunned again, their crude words spat like gunfire into the air. The truck lurched forward with an ear-splitting squeal of tires.

Heading straight for him.

Heath didn't move. A small voice inside him whispered, "This is it. Let it happen. Stand still and it will all be over."

It was tempting, that voice, inviting as it tugged at the shards of his heart still beating. All he had to do was not move, that was all.

He held his breath, letting it happen, feeling time slow the same way a movie did when the slow-motion button was hit on the remote. His senses sharpened. The rain tapped against his face with a keen punch and slid along his skin. So wet and cold.

The wind blew through him as if he were already gone. His chest swelled as he breathed in one last time. He smelled the distinct sweetness of wet hay from some farmer's field and the petroleum exhaust from the truck. The headlights speeding toward him bore holes into his retinas.

Just don't move. It was what he wanted with all his being. He felt the swish of the next moment, although it hadn't happen yet. The truck gaining speed, the squealing tires and the stillness within him as he wished for an end to his pain.

But even the wish was wrong. He knew it. His spirit bruised with the sin of it. At the last moment he sidestepped, the same moment the pickup veered right and careened off into the rain. Time shot forward, the rain fell with a vengeance and his lungs burned with the cold. He listened to the subwoofers thumping as the truck vanished.

Lightning split the sky. The sudden brightness seared his eyes and cleaved through his lost soul, and then he was plunged into darkness again.

Alive. He was still alive.

Wind drove icy rain against him like a boat at sea and wet him to the skin. Water sluiced down his face as he stood, shivering from the cold and a pain so deep it had broken him. Being alive was no victory. He felt that death would have been kinder. But not by his own choice and, once again, hopelessness drowned him.

"Are you all right?" Her concern came sharp and startling as the thunder overhead.

Heath turned toward her, like a blind man pivoting toward the sound that could save him. But nothing could. Lost and alone, he was aware of what he must look like to her. His clothes were soaked through. His hair clung to his scalp and forehead. Rain dripped off the tip of his nose and the cleft in his chin.

There, in the cheerful glow of the diner's windowed front, the two women stood framed in the light. Two women, one a half inch or so taller than the other, with blond hair pulled back from nearly identical faces. They had to be related. The classic features of girl-next-door good looks ought to be a re-assuring sight.

Except both women were watching him with horror-filled eyes. He must look like a nut.

With the darkness tugging him and the brutal rain beating him back, he ducked his head and plowed into the storm. He splashed through puddles and the water seeped through the hole in his left boot. As he went, his big toe became wetter and his sock began to wick water across to his other toes.

"Goodness, you gave us a scare!" The waitress was holding the door for him. Concern made her seem to glow as the light haloed her.

He blinked, and the effect was gone.

Maybe it was from his fatigue or the fact that adrenaline had kicked in and was tremulous in his veins. He still had the will to live, after all.

Thunder crashed like giant cymbals overhead, and it felt as if he broke with it. As he trudged up the steps and into the heat of the diner, bitterness filled him. There was shelter from this storm, but not from the one that had ripped apart his life.

No, there was no rest and no sanctuary from the past. Not tonight.

The waitress moved aside as he shouldered by, and he felt her intake of breath. The concern was still there, for she wore it like the apron over her jeans and blouse. As sincere as it was, he had no use for concern or sympathy. Those paltry emotions were easy to put on and take off and the words, "I'm sorry for your loss" came back to him.

Words meant to comfort him, when for a fact they were for the speaker's benefit. To make the speaker feel safe from the brutal uncertainty this life sometimes had to offer.

He'd learned it the hard way. Life played tricks with a person. Get too much, become too happy and bam! It could all disappear in the space between one second and the next.

It was a lesson he would never forget and he doubted the pretty waitress with her big blue-violet eyes and lustrous ponytail of gold would ever understand. What tragedy could happen here in this small little burgh miles from frantic big cities and desperation?

None, that's what. His boots squished and squeaked against the tile floor as he ambled down the aisle. The faint scent of perfume stayed with him, something subtle and sweet that made him think of dewy violets at dawn's first light and of hope. *That's* what that fragrance smelled like, and he wanted nothing to do with hope.

He didn't look back as he lumbered the length of the diner to the booth where his burger waited. He reached into his back pocket and hauled out his wallet. Dropped a ten on the table. "I've changed my mind. I want this to go."

"Sure thing."

She'd said that phrase before and just like that. Politely cheery words held up like a shield as she efficiently went about her work. Amy, her little gold nametag said. Amy. She didn't look like an Amy. Amys were cute and sweet and bubbly, and this one was somber. Polite and nice, but somber. She liked to keep people at a distance. He knew enough about shields to recognize one when he saw it. He had too many of his own.

She returned with a container and he took it from her. He didn't like to be waited on. He tipped his plate and the burger and fries tumbled into the box.

Ever efficient, the waitress reached into her crisp apron pocket and laid a handful of ketchup packets on the table. That annoyed him. He couldn't say why. Maybe because he felt her gaze. Her heavy, questioning gaze as if she were trying to take his measure. Trying to figure him out.

He'd given up long ago.

"There's no charge," her voice followed him like a light in a bleak place. "For what you tried to do."

"I pay my own way."

Whatever kind of man he looked like, he had standards. He had pride. He had no use for handouts. He wasn't looking for a soup kitchen and a quick revival meeting to patch up the holes in his soul.

He doubted even God could do that. So he faced the storm. What was a little wind and rain? Nothing.

He was so numb inside that he didn't feel the icy rain streaking in rivulets along the back of his neck. He didn't feel the water squish into his boot as he crossed the unlit parking lot and became part of the chill and the night.

Chapter Two

"What's with you?" Rachel asked as she tied off a bulging black garbage sack. "You're attacking that floor as if it's your own personal enemy."

Amy put a little more shoulder power into the mop. The yellow sponged head compressed into a flat line, oozing soap bubbles as she wrenched the handle back and forth. "I'm trying to get the floor clean."

"Yeah, but we don't want the tile to come off with the dirt."

She had a point, Amy realized as she gave up on the faintest of black streaks—she'd need to buff those out. Otherwise the floor sparkled. She dunked the mop into the bucket, surrendering, and rubbed at the small of her aching back. "Is this day over yet?"

"Go home. I can finish up."

"No, I told you I'd stay and I will. We leave together."

"What about Westin? He's waiting up for you. I don't have anyone at home for me. You go on."

"No. We share the work. And that's low, using my son to get me to do what you want." Amy loved her sister, who meant well. Who always gave too much. "You know I'm thinking of him."

Was it wrong that she was thinking of someone else, too?

Yes. Determined to sweep the lone stranger from her mind, she lugged mop and bucket to the industrial sink and, with a heave, emptied the dirty, soapy water. There. The bucket was clean and so was her...well, her list of distractions. Westin came first. Always first. She had no business thinking about some man whose name she didn't know.

Men always led to trouble. Sure, there were a few good ones in the world, but they were as rare as hen's teeth, as her grandmother used to say. And you couldn't always tell the mettle of a man, no matter how wonderful he seemed, until it was too late.

That was the truth. There were so many things she wished she could go back in time and change. She'd right every mistake and every problem that had blown up into a bigger problem.

But there was one thing she would never regret, and that was deciding to keep her son. It hadn't been easy for either of them, but they were a team, and somehow they'd get through this. With the good Lord's help. And, of course, her family's.

Rachel wrestled a second garbage bag out of the industrial-sized bin and tied it off. "If you want to trade shifts tomorrow, let me know. Or, if you need me to sit with him so you don't have to pay a baby-sitter, I'm available. You know how I love to spend time with my nephew."

"Thanks, I'll let you know. This means I'm doing the early-morning shift tomorrow?"

"Paige gets back in two days. We just have to survive until then."

Amy dumped a dollop of soap into the bucket and ran fresh hot water. "Survive? I think we're doing really good on our own."

"Except for the short-handed part."

Paige was their older sister, who ran everything perfectly and was out of town. And while chaperoning the youth-group trip to the Grand Canyon was great, no one had known ahead of time that the cook was going to up and quit out of the blue and leave them shuffling to fill his position and cover most of Paige's duties.

Rachel, her soft heart showing, straightened from garbage detail. "You've been working way more shifts than I have. I know, you don't mind. You can use the extra tip money. Speaking of which, please take me up on my offer to baby-sit. I know you think it'll be imposing, but I really want to help. I'm supposed to spend tomorrow doing the books, so it's done for Paige's inspection when she gets back. I can just take everything over to your place. Maybe alternate posting to the ledgers with playing a few games, video and otherwise."

There was no way Amy could say no to her sister's big doe eyes. And Rachel knew it. Not to mention it would help with the baby-sitter's bill. But that wasn't the driving reason she agreed. "I'm sure Westin would love to spend his day with his Aunt Rachel. He's been wanting to play Candyland with you."

"Oh, that's my very favorite game. Probably because I've always had a sweet tooth." Rachel cheerfully grabbed the bulging garbage bags, one in each hand. She was gone with a slap of the door.

Thunder cannoned overhead, echoing in the empty dining room. Amy rocked back on her heels. Wow, that was a good one. As she turned off the faucet and hefted the bucket from the sink, her heart went out to her son miles away. Had he heard it, too? He didn't like storms.

I'll be home as soon as I can, baby. Just one patch of floor left. Moving fast, she leaned the mop against the wall and hustled down the aisle, flipping the chairs onto tabletops as she went.

She stopped at the last booth. It was where *he'd* sat. The stranger. The image of him remained as brightly as if he'd been on a movie screen, how he'd stood with feet braced and shoulders wide in the rain. How he'd faced down the oncoming blaze of headlights and refused to move. He was either really brave or he had a death wish, and she'd nearly fainted with horror watching as the truck had careened toward him. Certain he was about to be hit, she'd started running toward the door until, at the last moment, he'd stepped out of harm's way.

Then, as if he'd done nothing of consequence, he growled at her, refused her thanks and left the diner with his meal in hand. He just stalked out the door, eager to be on his way, solitary and remote.

Wasn't that just like a man?

Oh, well, he was gone. She wished him luck. She didn't know what else to do. She would add him to her prayer list tonight. He'd made her feel things she'd worked hard to keep buried. Feelings and memories she'd banished after her son was born and she'd come home a different woman from the girl who'd left for big-city excitement with a chip on her shoulder and something to prove—only to find out that home wasn't as bad as she'd thought.

The back door blew open and slammed against the wall. Rachel came in with the wind and rain. "Whew. It nearly blew me away out there and it's getting worse. Let's hightail it out of here while we can."

"I'm almost done." Determined to finish, Amy upended the final chair. Something dark tumbled to the floor.

She knelt to retrieve it. Mercy's A's was scrawled in worn gold-and-white letters on the black fabric of a man's baseball hat. The bill had curved into a sagging humped shape as if from years of wear. Her loner had sat at this table, but had he been wearing a hat? She didn't remember one.

It had been a busy day and a busier evening rush. Anyone could have left that cap any time during the supper hours, but there was something about it that made her think of him. Maybe it was the color; her loner had been wearing black.

Her loner—that's how she was thinking of him, as if she knew him. Maybe it was that she recognized a part of herself in the man. Maybe because she understood it wasn't only courage but something stronger that had made him stand motionless staring down death.

Yeah, she recognized the feel of despair that clung to him. She knew a like soul when she saw it.

She stowed the cap in the lost-and-found

box, tucked it beneath the cash register and got back to work. Rachel was clattering around in the back office—it was little more than a closet, which it had been years and years ago when their parents had run the place.

But after their death, Paige had taken over and decided the front counter was no place to work on the books. So she'd checked out a how-to guide from the library and put them all to work. Amy had chosen the soft yellow paint because it was her favorite color. Of course, she was nine years old at the time. Now the color only reminded her of times best left forgotten. So she was happy to finish the mopping while Rachel muttered about over-rings in the cramped little office.

Amy glanced at the clock—ten thirty-eight—before rapping on the door, which was open. All she saw was Rachel's back as she hunched over the plywood desk built into the back wall. That didn't look comfortable. "I'm done out here. Is there anything I can do to help?"

"Nope. This tape is a mess. I need to talk to whichever of the twins did this today." Frustrated, Rachel slid back in the folding metal chair and rubbed her forehead with both hands. "Those two are giving me a serious headache."

Their teenaged cousins were not the most faultless of employees, but they were eager and worked hard. "They just have a lot to learn."

"I know." Rachel's sigh spoke more of her own tiredness than of her upset at the girls, who had both turned seventeen last month. "I'm just going to throw all this in a bag and take it home. I'll make the deposit tomorrow."

"Sounds good to me."

The lights blinked off and stayed off. Pitch black echoed around them.

Amy didn't move. "It looks like we lost power. Do you think it's off for good?"

It stayed dark. That seemed like answer enough. Amy was trying to remember where the flashlights were when Rachel's chair creaked and it was followed by the rasp of a drawer opening. A round beacon of light broke through the inky blackness. Leave it to Rachel. Amy breathed easier. At least they'd be able to close up without feeling their way in the dark.

Lightning flashed, and immediately thunder crashed like breaking steel overhead. Closer. The front was coming fast and moving toward home. She thought of her little boy. Westin was safe with the baby-sitter, but he'd be worried. She couldn't call to reassure him. It wasn't safe with the lightning crackling overhead and besides, if the power was out, then the phone lines were probably down, too.

She grabbed her purse from the shelf and her jacket hanging next to it, working in the near dark, for Rachel was hogging the flashlight to zip the cash receipts and the day's take into her little leather briefcase. Once that was done, Amy hurried ahead and re-checked the front door—locked, just as it was supposed to be—and followed the sound of Rachel tapping through the kitchen toward the back door.

Outside seemed just as dark. An inky blackness was broken only when lightning strobed overhead and speared into the fields just out of town. It was definitely heading south. All she wanted to do was to get home before a tree or a power line blocked the road out of town.

She manhandled the door closed and turned the key in the dead bolt. The wind whipped and lashed at her, strong enough to send her stumbling through the puddles. In the space between lightning bolts, she could feel the electric charge on her skin. It came crisp and metallic in the air.

Rain came in a rage and it bounced like golf balls over the battered blacktop lot and over them. She hadn't gone two yards and she was drenched to the skin. Following the faint glow of Rachel's flashlight, she let the wind hurl her toward two humps of shadows that became two parked cars as they stumbled closer. The windshields gleamed, reflecting the finger of fire sizzling overhead. Lightning snapped into a power pole a block or two away. The thunder boomed so hard, Amy's eardrums hurt with the shock.

Maybe that's why she didn't see another shadow until headlights flashed to life. She recognized the row of piercing fog lights blazing atop a pickup's cab. Oh, heavens. It was the two men who'd hassled her in the restaurant.

It happened so fast. The truck screeched to a halt inches from Rachel, who'd been in the lead. The passenger door thrust open and suddenly there he was, the dark form of a stocky man, muscled arms held out with his hands closed into fists. Everything about him screamed danger. He stalked toward Rachel like a coyote ready to strike.

Amy didn't remember making the choice to fight instead of run. She was simply there, between the man and her sister. Protective anger made her feel ten feet tall. "Get out of here. Now."

"Hey, that's no way to talk. I just wanted to give you girls a chance to make back your five bucks. Maybe even earn a tip." The strong scent of hard liquor wafted from him.

She wasn't afraid; she was mad. "That's a horrible thing to say. Shame on you. You get back in your truck and leave us alone, or I'll—"

"Yeah, what are you gonna do, pretty lady?" he mocked, and then the smirk faded from his shadowed face.

For out of the black curtain of rain emerged another man. One who stood alone.

Maybe it was the glaze of light snaking across the sky behind him. Or the way his dark hair lashed in the wind, but he looked like a warrior legend come to life. There was no mistaking the sheer masculine steel of the man as his presence seemed to silence the thunder.

He didn't utter a word. He didn't need to. The look of him—iron-strong and defensive—made the troublemaker shrink back as if he'd been struck. The ruffian cast one hard look at Amy—she saw the glint of malice before he leaped into the cab and slammed the door. The truck shot through the downpour, roaring out of sight.

Amy realized she was trembling from the inside out, now that the threat was gone. She swiped the rain from her eyes. She didn't know why some people behaved the way they did. As long as Rachel was safe. They were both safe. She remembered to send a note of thanks heavenward.

And her loner her protector—waited, his back to them, his feet braced wide, his fists on his hips looking as invincible as stone as he watched in the direction of the road, as if making sure those troublemakers weren't doubling back.

"Oh, I can't believe those men! If you can call them men." Rachel walked on wobbly legs toward her car. "I've got to sit down."

"They scared me, too." Amy opened her sister's car door and took the keys from her trembling hand. She sorted through them for the ignition key as Rachel collapsed onto the seat.

"Are you all right?"

Amy turned at the sound of his voice, rough like the thunder and as elemental as the wind.

He was simply a man, not legend or myth, but with the way he looked unbowed by the rain and lashed by the storm, he gave the presence of more.

When he spoke, it was as if the world silenced. "He didn't hurt you, did he? I came across the parking lot as fast as I could."

But from where? Amy wondered. He could have come out of the very night, for he seemed forged out of the clouds and dark. She swiped a hand across her brow, trying to get the rain out of her eyes and saw the faint glaze of lightning reflecting in the windows far down the alley. The town's only motel. That's where her loner had come from.

"You arrived just in time," she assured him, standing to block the rain for her sister. "We're all right."

"Thanks to you. Again." Rachel was still clutching the briefcase to her chest.

Amy knew what she was thinking. Rachel had their day's take tucked in her leather case. It was a lot to lose, had the men been interested in money only.

"You ladies want me to call the sheriff?" The loner kept his stance and his distance like a protective wolf standing on the edge of a forest, ready to slip back in.

"No, it looks like the phone lines are down, too. I'll stop by and see the deputy. I drive right by his place on my way home—"

Lightning flashed like stadium floodlights, eerily illuminating the parking lot and the three of them drenched with rain. Thunder exploded instantly and a tree limb on the other side of the alley crashed to the ground, smoking.

The rain increased so she had to shout to be heard. "This is dangerous. Get inside. I'll—"

She didn't get to finish her invitation for breakfast in the diner. The lightning returned and made every surface of her skin prickle. Here she was, standing up in the parking lot, and how dangerous was that? She yanked her car door open and dove into the seat, grateful for the shelter. Through the rain-streaked windshield, she could see her loner in the parking lot, a dark silhouette the storm seemed to revolve around.

Rain hammered harder, sluicing so fast down the glass she lost sight of him. When the water thinned for a second, he was gone. There was only wind and rain where he'd stood.

Good. He'd returned to his motel room, where he'd be safe. The car windows began fogging and she realized her fingers were like ice, so she started the engine and flipped the defroster on high.

In the parking spot beside her, Rachel's old sedan came to life, too, the high beams bright as she put the car in gear, creeping forward as if to make sure Amy was okay.

Amy wasn't okay, but she knew her sister wasn't going to drive off and leave her sitting here. So she buckled up and put the car in gear. She ignored the groan of the clutch because it needed to be replaced and, after creeping forward, realized she needed both the wipers and the lights on.

Rachel's car moved away and Amy followed her, steering through the downpour that came ever harder. But her gaze drifted to the rearview, where the motel ought to be. She couldn't see it; there was only darkness. Remembering the loner and the way he'd stood as if he were already not a part of this world, she wished...she didn't know what she wished. That he would find rest for whatever troubled him.

She would always be grateful he'd stepped between her and possible danger twice. Lord knew there had been times when that wasn't always the case.

The rain pummeled so hard overhead, she couldn't hear the melody of the Christian country station or the beat of the wipers on high as she let the storm blow her home.

"Mom!"

The instant Amy had stumbled through the front door, she'd been caught by her son. His arms vised her waist, and he held on tight, clinging for moments longer than his usual welcome-home hug as thunder cannoned over the roof and shook the entire trailer.

Oh, her sweet little boy, the shampoo scent of him, fresh from his bath, and the fabric softener in his astronaut pjs just made her melt. She feathered her fingers through his rich brown hair the color of milk chocolate and when he let go, he didn't look scared. But his chin was up and his little hands balled tight. Westin was great at hiding everything, true to his gender.

Only she knew how storms scared him. The hitch in his breathing told her his asthma medicine was working. The image from earlier today of the needle pricking along his spine tore at her. Her little one had had a rough day, and she remembered how he'd set his jaw tight and not made a sound. Tears had welled in his eyes but he hadn't let them fall.

Her tough little guy.

She knelt to draw him against her. "I figured you'd be sound asleep by now and I wouldn't get to read you another chapter in your story like I promised."

"The thunder kept wakin' me up. It's loud. So I just stayed awake."

That was his excuse. Tough as nails, just like her dad had been. Every time she looked at him, she saw it, the image of her father, a hint that always made her remember the man who'd been twenty feet tall for her. Who could do anything.

There were the little things Westin did that would twist like a knife carved deep. In the innocent gestures, as he was doing now, chin up, arms crossed in front of his chest, all warrior. Tough on the outside, soft as butter on the inside. Yeah, he was just like her dad.

"Okay, tiger, it's way past your bedtime. Get to your room and under your covers. I'll be back in half a second."

His big brown eyes stared up at her. She caught the flash of fear when it sounded as if golf balls were hitting the roof with the force of a hurricane, but she nodded, letting him know without words that she was here now. He might be cowboy-tough, but he was a little boy who needed his mother. She wouldn't let anything hurt her little one.

"'Kay," he agreed, "but hurry up! We got a light all set up and everything. Bye, Kelly!" he called to the woman in the shadows of the tiny kitchen.

"G'night, don't let the bedbugs bite!" came the answer and then her cousin by marriage emerged from the dark with her coat in hand. Kelly slipped one arm into the raincoat's sleeve and then the other. "Hi, Amy. I got the dishes put away, too, just to help out. If you want me tomorrow night, just give me a call. You know I can use the extra cash."

"Sure." Amy dug through her apron pocket and counted out a small stack of ones. Tips had been sparse with the state economy the way it was and they'd been even worse tonight.

She regretted that three-quarters of her tip money was already gone, but there were other places to cut corners. Her son's care was not one of them. "Rachel wants to come over and spend time with him tomorrow, but if I have to work at night, I'll give you a call. We're still short-handed. Are you sure you don't want a job at the diner?"

"It's harder to do my school work and wait tables at the same time. I have a test Monday." Kelly settled her backpack on one shoulder. It was heavy with college texts and notebooks.

Amy had wanted to attend college, too, like so many of her friends and cousins had. Sparkling-eyed freshmen going to classes and chatting over coffee and learning exciting new things. There were a lot of reasons that had kept her from that path, mostly her own choices and the fact that a college education took money neither she nor her family had.

She admired Kelly for sticking to the hard course. It couldn't be easy working several jobs and studying, too. "Drive safe out there. The roads are slick."

"I will. Heavens!" Kelly opened the door and the racket was deafening.

Hail punched the pavement and hammered off the row of trailers lined up in neat order along the dark street. Ice gleamed black as it hid lawns and driveways and flowerbeds starting to bloom.

The wind gusted and Amy wrestled the door closed. She pulled the little curtain aside and watched through the window in the door, making sure Kelly got to her car safely and it started all right. In a town where few people ever bothered to lock anything, Amy turned the dead bolt and made sure Kelly made it safely down the lane.

It's just the storm, she told herself. That's why she felt unsettled. But she knew that wasn't the truth.

The hail echoed like continual gunshots

through the single wide, and she circled the living room, dodging the couch. A thick candle, one she'd gotten for Christmas, sat in the center of the coffee table and shed enough light for her to see her way around an array of toy astronauts and space ships arranged in the middle of a battle. The windows were cold, streaked with ice and rain and locked up tight.

Amy knew it wasn't the storm that bothered her. It was those two men tonight. The harsh, brash way they'd laughed over their meal. The suggestive leers they'd shot at her. The way they'd walked out of the diner without fully paying, as if they had the right. It all burned in her stomach, the anger and the helplessness of it. They probably thought nothing of it, just two guys out having some fun.

But it was a big deal, their lack of respect. She wasn't some questionable woman. She had standards and morals she lived by. What hurt is that times like this and men like that reminded her of the days when she'd behaved in ways she deeply regretted.

Don't think about it. It's over and done with now. She'd do best to erase the entire experience from her mind. She'd told the incident to the deputy on her way home. He lived four doors down. He was on his way out on an emergency call, but he told her he'd be by the diner in the morning if she wanted to file a report. She didn't. There was no point. Things like that were public record and she wanted to keep as far away from the ugliness of the outside world as she could. For her son, and for herself.

This trailer wasn't much, but it was hers and she'd worked hard to make the best of it. The tan shag carpeting was nothing fancy, but it was freshly vacuumed and in good repair. She'd laid it herself, after buying it as a remnant from a flooring outlet store in Bozeman.

Last year she'd retextured the walls in the living room and applied several coats of the lightest blue paint. The couch had been in the family for what seemed like generations. She'd reupholstered it and made the throw pillows that cheerfully matched the walls. Pretty lace curtains—she'd made a good yard-sale find with those—hung on decorative rods she'd mounted and gave the cozy room a sense of softness.

This was her sanctuary, and Westin's boyhood home. She breathed in the serenity and felt more centered. She knelt to blow out the candle, and darkness washed over her. Tonight the shadows did not seem as peaceful. Hail echoed through the spaces and corners of the trailer and filled her with trepidation, as if the past could rear up and snatch away her life here.

I'm just tired, that's all. Amy rose, breathing in the faint smoke rising off the wick and peppermint-scented wax. The uneasiness remained.

"Mom!" Westin stood in the wash of light from his bedroom door, looking like a waif in pjs that were a size too big. He was holding his stuffed Snoopy by the ear.

Her heart broke. Why was she letting the unease from the past trouble her? There was no reason to look back. She'd come a long way, and she'd done it all by herself—okay, with the help of God and her sisters. Westin was waiting for her, and no way was she going to let him down.

"Are your teeth brushed?" she asked, because it was her job as a mom.

"Kelly made me."

"And what about your prayers?"

"Yep. I told ya. I'm really, really ready."

"Then get into bed, young man. Hurry up."

He ran, feet pounding as he raced out of her sight. The squeak of the box spring told her he'd jumped onto his mattress and was bouncing around, all boy energy, even this late at night.

If only she could harness it, she thought wistfully, as she bent her aching back to blow out the other candle on the little dinette set in the eating nook. Every bone in both feet seemed to groan and wince as she headed down the hall, drawn through the darkness by the light in her little boy's room.

Westin was waiting and ready, tucked beneath his covers. A candle in a stout holder—Kelly must have placed it there—shone brightly enough on the pillow to reveal the boy's midnight-blue bedspread with the planets sprinkled all over it. The rings of Saturn. The storms of Jupiter. The icy moon of…Jupiter? She couldn't keep straight which moons belonged to which planets, but she should know it by heart because it was nearly all Westin talked about.

"Kelly and I saved the chapter on black

holes for you to read, Mom!" Big blue eyes sparkling, Westin hid a cough in his fist and scrunched back into the pillows. Snoopy, clenched tightly in the crook of one arm, was apparently anticipating the wealth of information on black holes, too.

"I've been looking forward to this all day." Amy settled onto the bedside and held the heavy library book open in her hands. The spine cracked, the plastic cover crinkled and she breathed in the wonderful scent of books, paper and ink. She cleared her throat and began to read.

As exciting as gravity was, and as awesome as it was to hear about some stars exploding their matter into space, while others sank into themselves, Westin's eyelids flickered. He yawned hugely and fought hard to stay awake. When she got to the part about gravity sucking light and matter into the net of a black hole, Westin's lids stayed shut. His jaw relaxed. Snoopy kept watching her, however.

She slipped a bookmark between the pages and set the book on the nightstand. She just watched her son sleep for a few minutes with her heart full. Then she rose, blew out the candle and shut his door tightly.

The hall was pitch-black. Hail still rattled against the walls. Listening to the wind groan, Amy slipped into the darkness of her room. There was a tiny reading light, run on battery power, on her headboard. She unclipped it and flicked it on. It was a faint light and not strong enough to scare away the deep shadows from the room.

The uneasiness was still inside her. It was the loner. Tonight he'd somehow breached the careful shield she kept around her. Maybe it wasn't that he'd broken through her defenses as much as she saw through his. And what she saw there reminded her of hard lessons she'd learned.

When a person lost her innocence, there was no way to get it back—even if she surrounded herself with family and friends, lived in a small rural town where she'd lived nearly all her life, where she knew everyone, where nothing bad hardly ever happened.

She could work hard, do her very best, pay her bills on time, make a home, raise a son and sometimes, like tonight, there would be something that would remind her.

Some wounds ran too deep to heal. And there lived within her a scar that cut into her soul. She was as lost as the loner had seemed to be. And as wounded.

In the dark, alone in her room, she felt revealed. In an act just short of desperation, she switched on the clock radio by her bed and forgot the lights were out. Tonight there would be no soothing twang of familiar Christian songs to lull away some of the void.

She hurried about her bedtime routine, the little habits reassuring her, making her feel as if everything was in its place. She washed her face, flossed, brushed her teeth, smoothed cream on those little lines beside her eyes and mouth. She changed into her soft flannel pajamas and knelt to say her prayers.

The storm was moving on. The hail turned to rain as she crawled under the covers, and then to silence.

But it wasn't a peaceful silence.

Chapter Three

Heath growled in frustration from beneath the pillow that he'd wedged over his head. But it wasn't working to block out first light.

It was his brand of luck. His motel room faced east—and that meant bright searing sunlight was finding its way through the gaps in the fifty-year-old curtain, and it lit up the place like a lighthouse's beacon. The light seemed to pulse and dance because the old heater that clattered like a hamster running on a squeaky wheel all night long and wouldn't turn off, was spewing hot air full-blast beneath the curtains.

Oh yeah, it was another night in a long string of countless nights without much sleep to speak of. His eyes were gritty, his mind numb and his back muscles aching from the sagging mattress. By the time he'd stepped into the shower, he was already resigned and so the fact that the water stayed cold even when he'd turned the knob to full force hot didn't bother him so much.

These days not much did. His single duffel bag was ready to go and waiting by the door. He never bothered to unpack. When he was dried off and dressed, he tossed his toothbrush and half-rolled tube of toothpaste into the bag's side pocket. He then added his unused razor. He scraped a hand over his two-day stubble—not too long to itch yet and he didn't care if he looked a little on the scruffy side.

He squinted into the mirror as he zipped up the duffel. The man who looked back at him had the weary look of a drifter. The worn-down-to-the-nub soul he'd seen in so many of the homeless men he'd treated when they had stumbled into his emergency room.

He winced. Any thoughts of his old life brought up the beginnings of a pain so black, it would drown him. Or, maybe it already had, he reasoned as he looked away from the man in the mirror and slung the battered bag over his shoulder.

The stranger staring back at him didn't resemble Dr. Heath Murdock, not in any way. He was no longer the vascular surgeon with a specialty in trauma medicine, who could handle any crisis, any unspeakable catastrophe with the calm steady confidence of a man born to save lives.

What he couldn't stand to think about were the lives he'd failed to save.

So he headed out into the morning and welcomed the crisp bite to the early-spring air. The cheerful sun burned his eyes. Blinking hard, he ambled along the cracked sidewalk, uneven from the towering maples lining the parking lot, their roots exposed like old arthritic fingers digging into the dirt.

Head down, he dropped the room key off at the front desk where a tired woman in brown polyester mumbled thanks without looking up at him. He saw a home dye job and graying roots. The deep creases in the woman's face were testimony of too many decades of hard living and heartbreak.

Yeah, he knew. He unlocked the passenger door of the old pickup. The truck used to be his granddad's. Faint memories of sunny days riding around the Iowa farm with his grandpop washed through him.

Good times. Times he could tolerate thinking about. He dropped the duffel on the passenger floor, where decades of boots had worn scuffs. Tiny bits of straw and dried grass seed remained dug deep into the grooves around the door. The distant voices of long ago echoed for one brief moment—*Grandpop, when I grow up I'm gonna be just like you!... Lord I hope so, son, 'cuz there ain't nothin' better than bein' a cowboy.*

The voices silenced as he slammed the door hard and breathed in the scented air.

There was hay and alfalfa growing next door in fields that rolled out of sight. The faint scent of irrigation made him feel like breathing in a little more deeply. When he pulled out his wallet, there were no pictures inside and no credit cards. There was nothing but a driver's license and insurance card and, tucked between the two, his social security number.

Not that the jobs he'd been working lately had required legal ID.

He checked the thin bills—forty-six bucks left. That wouldn't get him far. Looked like it was time to think about working for a while. This town with dust settling on the main drag through town—only one pickup had bothered to drive past this early in the morning—didn't look like a hopping place… and that was just about his speed these days.

Across the parking lot he recognized an older model compact car, neat and clean and familiar. The waitress. He watched as she hopped out of the vehicle. She was wearing jeans and a red T-shirt that was baggy more than it was form-fitting. Her long blond hair was still damp from a shower and dancing on the breeze.

He watched her, unable to look away, as she took two steps toward the back door, skidded to a halt on black tennis shoes, and spun. She scurried back to her car, muttering to herself as if in great frustration. She hadn't locked her car, so it took only a moment to yank it open. Then she bent down and he couldn't see her beneath the door.

He leaned his forearms on the truck bed and watched as she bobbed up into sight. Her hair was more disheveled and she was muttering harder to herself as if she were having a very bad morning. This time she had a small tan purse in a death grip as she paced across the parking lot, looking as if she was working up a good head of steam. Yeah, he used to have mornings like that—

In a flash, it was right at the edge of his mind, the days of rushing out of the house, leaving too much behind him undone and two shadows in the doorway he couldn't let himself see even in memory. Breaking into pieces, he slammed the door on the past and locked it well. Some things a man couldn't live through.

Not that he was alive. Only his heart was beating, that was all.

He hung his head, hidden behind the pickup as he heard the waitress's rapid gait stop in midstride. He peered through his lashes, not lifting his head, to see her hesitate, looking around as if she felt him there, felt him watching her. But she didn't spot him. Was she remembering last night and feeling jumpy? Any woman would. He hadn't meant to make her uneasy, he just didn't want to talk to her. He didn't want a lot of things.

Maybe there was another place to eat in town.

He followed the alley to the front street.

On the far side of the empty two-lane road, a train rumbled along the tracks hauling a long string of box containers. The bright black-and-blue paint of inner-city graffiti marked the sides of the cars, heading west, probably to the ports of Seattle or Portland.

Portland. He wondered why he even let that word into his mind.

A lone pickup, vintage fifties model, perfectly restored in a grass-green and shining chrome rolled down the street and pulled into a spot directly in front of the diner. The Open sign in the front window and the door open wide to the morning was invitation enough.

The man who climbed down from the pickup's seat without bothering to lock up as he loped up onto the sidewalk looked to be a retired farmer. There was the look of a hard-working man to him, lean, trim and efficient. Gray-white hair fringed the blue cap he wore.

He pushed through the screen door that slapped behind him and voices rose from inside the restaurant.

"That's what I like to see, coffee waiting...."

A woman's lilting laughter answered.

It was all Heath could hear before a puff of

wind changed direction, taking the words away. In the glint of the sparkling front window, Heath could see into the diner. He watched the man take a booth at the front window, his coffee cup full and already waiting for him. A regular customer? He probably showed up every morning now that he no longer had a farm to tend and ordered the same breakfast.

It was early yet, but the rest of the main street—which was what, only four blocks long?—was as dark as could be. The only other sign of life was the flash of a neon sign newly blazing on a quaint coffee shop on the corner. Drive-through Open, it announced in cheerful blue letters.

Heath's stomach rumbled as he debated what to do.

The whisper of a car approaching on the road had him turning around. There was no mistaking the big gray cruiser with the mounted red and blue lights and the emblem on the doors. The local law had arrived. The passenger window whispered down as the car pulled up alongside the curb. Behind the wheel was a man in uniform, as fit and as steely as only a marine could be.

Recognizing his own kind, Heath gave a salute. "Is there a problem, sir?"

From inside the cruiser, the uniformed deputy gave him a cursory look and, finding him satisfactory, saluted him in return. "We don't get a lot of out-of-towners this time of day. Need some help, soldier?"

"I can find my way, sir." His years in the military—there was a time Heath didn't mind remembering.

His service in the first Desert Storm had done more than change his life. It had made him know the true meaning of being a man. And what medicine was all about. Individuals. People. Not five years spent afterwards in one of the best hospitals in the country could change the integrity he'd learned in service to this country.

It was the only thing holding him together.

The deputy cracked a grin. "I was Marine Recon."

"I was the doc that patched up your kind. You Special Forces guys seem to get into trouble on a regular basis."

"I let a few of you sawbones work on me a time or two. I blame the ache in my arm on those docs. It couldn't have been the two bullets and grenade shrapnel I caught. You wouldn't happen to be the customer Amy McKaslin was tellin' me about last night. You stopped her and her sister from bein' hassled?"

"I didn't do much. I just showed up. Did she get their license plate?"

"No. You didn't happen to—"

Heath recited it from memory. "You look those boys up. The way they acted, it was no way to treat two real nice women."

"Exactly." The deputy reached for his radio. "You wouldn't object to making a statement, would ya? I don't take well to women being threatened in my town."

"They skipped out on part of their bill, too." Heath saw the lift of surprise of the officer's brow, and knew the waitress hadn't told the whole story. Probably because it was a matter of five dollars. "I'll sign whatever you need me to."

"Drop by the office after you're done eating. It's down past the hardware and keep going. You'll see us." With another salute, the deputy drove on.

Heath felt a ghost from the past—it was his own spirit. The man he used to be: whole and full of optimism and enthusiasm. Full of heart.

There wasn't much left of that man. He didn't recognize his reflection in the diner's windows. He merely saw a man who looked more tired and aged instead of a vibrant, driven marine. He was like any man about to patronize a typical diner in a typical rural American town.

A bubbly waitress—not Amy—led him to the table in the back. It suited him. He had a view of the train still rolling by like an endless caravan. He ordered the special—whatever, he didn't care—and thanked the waitress for handing him a local paper.

In his reflection in the window he caught sight of a man he used to know, just for one moment, and then it was gone like the train, the caboose slithering away and leaving a clear view of the park across the street. He stared for a long moment at the lush green grass waving in the wind.

The waitress returned with a carafe of steaming coffee, poured his cup full and dashed off with her sneakers squeaking on the clean tile. The coffee was black, had a bitter bite, and he drank it straight. He enjoyed the punch of caffeine.

He turned to the classified ads and browsed through them. The waitress returned with a huge plate stacked high with sunny-side-up eggs, sausage links, pancakes and hash browns. Just the sight of it brought back memories of his grandma's kitchen, where the syrup was the real thing and the jam homemade.

"Do you need anything else?" the waitress asked, producing a bottle of—just as he'd predicted—real maple syrup and a canning jar of what looked like blueberry preserves.

Before he could shake his head no, she was gone, rushing off to bring coffee to the new arrivals.

Alone in the corner, he ate until he was full. He felt like the outsider he was as more people arrived, friends greeted friends and family said hello to family. Cars began to crawl down the main street, mostly obeying the speed limit.

By the time kids were walking by on their way to school, Heath was done.

He pushed the empty plate and the newspaper away. There were no temporary jobs in the local paper. Maybe there'd be something in the next town along the highway. As for the blond waitress from last night, he wasn't disappointed over not seeing her again. He'd pay, leave a tip and be on his way. But would he think of her?

Yeah. He'd think of her. He couldn't say why as he headed down the aisle, past families and friends gathering, past conversations and everyday average human connections. There was something about the woman and it made him wonder...

No wondering, man. No wishing. He dropped a small stack of bills on the counter and pushed through the door.

Once again losing sight of the man he used to be, he ambled down the sidewalk. He was already thinking of moving on, as weightless as the wind.

Amy spotted long-time customer Bob Brisbane through the small window of the hand-off counter. The warmer lights cast a golden hue as she squinted through the opening, standing on tiptoe to see if he was alone. He was late this morning joining his buddies, who met every morning like clockwork to share gossip over breakfast, coffee and the morning paper.

Over the background music from the local inspirational station and the din of the busy diner, she could pick up Jodi's cheerful good morning as she poured Bob's coffee. As the two exchanged small talk of family and last night's storm, Amy cracked three eggs and whipped them in a bowl, with just enough milk and spices.

By the time Jodi had arrived with the order ticket, Amy already had the omelet sizzling next to a generous portion of link sausage and grated potatoes.

"Is that Mr. Winkler's order you've got nearly ready?"

"Yep, just need to add the bacon—" Amy used the spatula to lift the eight blackened strips of bacon, cooked just the way kindly Mr. Winkler liked it, and added it to his order of buttermilk pancakes and two poached eggs and handed up the plate. "I think I've almost caught up. Who knew it'd be such a busy morning?"

"It's the power outage. It sounds like nearly half the county was out of electricity

last night, and a lot are still out this morning."
Jodi bustled away with the order.

The noise in the dining room seemed to
crescendo, or maybe it was because she was
trying so hard to listen for the doorbell. She'd
hardly been able to sleep last night, for she
was troubled not only by the weather and the
stress of normal life, but also because she
couldn't get the loner out of her mind.

As she added plenty of cheese, smoked
sausage, onion and jalapeños to Mr. Brisbane's omelette—how anyone's stomach
could handle that at 6:23 a.m., she didn't
know—she thought of the loner again. Last
night rewound like a movie, to the place
where he'd stepped out of the storm, looking
more intimidating than the lightning forking
down to take out a transformer half a block
away.

By standing tall, he'd stopped whatever
those awful men had planned. She knew in her
heart he was leaving, maybe he'd already left,
but she had prayed he might stop in for breakfast before moving on. She'd been watching
for him between scrambling eggs and frying
bacon and browning potatoes and whipping
up her family's secret pancake recipe.

Had she seen him? No, of course not. She'd been busy, that was one problem, but there was only so much of the dining room she could see from behind the grill. Maybe he wasn't coming. He certainly didn't seem eager to see her last night. And she'd had the sinking feeling when he'd seemed to disappear in the storm that she'd never see him again. He'd more than likely followed the road out of town and she had responsibilities. People who counted on her. She ought to pay attention to her work—the omelet oozing melting cheese and the sausages nearly too brown.

She whisked the meat and eggs onto a clean dish, handed it up with her left hand as she turned bacon with the other. Wherever her loner was, she prayed the good he'd done for them was returned to him tenfold.

With the edge of the spatula, she scraped the grill—she liked a tidy kitchen—and studied the last meal ticket on the wheel. It looked like Mr. Whitley had shown up, the sixth member of the retired ranchers who met every morning at the same table. She cracked three eggs neatly—Mr. Redmond's Sunrise Special was the last of the first wave of the usual Saturday-morning rush. Maybe she'd be able to take a few minutes away from the grill, grab some coffee and—

Jodi shouldered through the doors, loaded down with empties, which she unloaded with sharp clatters at the sink. "Well, I tell you, that just about breaks my heart."

"I'm betting you don't mean the pile of dishes to clean?"

"Nope. I waited on a man this morning. Striking, young guy, somewhere around our age, maybe a bit older. You know how on some folks it's hard to tell?" She washed and yanked a paper towel from the dispenser to dry her hands.

Amy's pulse thickened. It was as if her blood had turned into sand, and her heart was straining to pump it through her veins. The background sounds of the cooking food and customers in the dining room faded to silence. Why was she reacting this strongly to the mere mention of the man?

Unaware, Jodi continued on. "Well, I tell ya, I've never seen a sadder-looking man. People got all kinds of heartaches, we both know that, but it just sort of clung to him like an aftershave or something. Just so much despair."

Amy knew. She'd seen it, too.

She tossed the used paper towel. "He looked like he was down to his last dollar, but he left me a five-dollar tip."

"You mean he was here and left?" *And I didn't see him?* The spatula clattered forgotten to the counter as she went up on tiptoe to peer at the long line of booths in front of the sunny window.

Of course he wasn't there, and she rocked back on her heels. "Finish this up, will you? I'll be right back."

"Well, sure, but what—?"

Amy pushed through the doors and left without answering. She hurried down the center aisle where old timers argued over politics and the weather, where early risers read the day's paper over coffee. A typical morning, with the scents and sounds and people she knew so well, and she couldn't explain why she felt so desperate. It was as if she'd failed to do something important, and that didn't make any sense at all.

The cap. She remembered, skidded to a stop in the doorway, let the glass door swing shut as she reversed and dropped behind the counter. The cap was still there on the top of the plastic bin and she grabbed it without thinking, pounding out the door, and making the bell jangle like a tambourine. Her shoes hit the pavement and the fresh breeze punched her face.

She ran half a block, past the diner and the drug store closed up tight. He was nowhere in sight. What was she doing running off like this? She'd left eggs on the grill. The sunshine slanted into her eyes, too bright to see up the sidewalk where it stretched the rest of the length of town. There was only one more block before buildings gave way to green pasture. He wasn't here. The hat probably wasn't his. So why was she standing here wanting something, and she didn't even know what it was.

What she should do was go back inside, rescue the Sunrise Special from the grill, concentrate on her job and not give the loner another thought. She didn't like men—she didn't trust them. She got along just fine in the world when they were customers or friends of the family or family. She had a policy against interacting with the male gender for any other reason. So, had she lost her senses, or what?

No, she was shivering in the brisk wind because of her conscience. Her faith taught the golden rule—to do unto others, and she had to thank him, if she could. Even if it was only to return his hat, *if* it was his hat.

A strange sensation skidded against her jaw and cheek, or maybe it was the trees whispering in the breeze. Either way, she turned toward the sensation and there was a man's dark form, a man dressed all in black, a shadow moving in the sun-bright alley.

It *was* him.

"Hey, wait up!" She started toward him, but the wind snatched her words and she feared he hadn't heard her. He kept on walking with his purposeful, leggy stride. She saw an older-model blue pickup, dusty and well used, parked at the motel's alley-side lot.

There. She had her answer. She firmly believed that the angels above wouldn't have brought him to her diner twice if there hadn't been a reason.

Determined, she jogged after him, with the cap clutched tight in her hand. "Hey! Mister!"

He had to have heard her this time. His brisk gait stiffened. His shoulders tensed to steel. His long athletic legs pumped notice-ably faster as he bridged the last few yards to the driver's door of his truck, unlocked the door and yanked it open. He was behaving as if he didn't want to talk with her. As if he wanted to avoid her.

She wasn't about to let a little thing like that get in her way. "Is this your cap?"

He turned, meeting her gaze through the window of the open cab door. His was a chilling look as he studied her from head to toe.

She was intensely aware of her scuffed sneakers and the knot in the right shoelace keeping it together as she jogged closer. As if resigned, he left the door open and backed away from the truck. A dark look masked his face. She held out the cap so he could read it.

He let out an exasperated sigh. "Yeah, it's mine."

"Good. Then I don't look quite so silly running after you at six-forty——" she glanced at her wristwatch "——seven in the morning."

"You don't look silly at all. Not at all. Just the opposite."

"Good. I try not to make a fool of myself before noon, at least." She held out the cap.

The sight of him in full light startled her.

He'd looked solemn and mighty in the night. By day he seemed taller than she'd figured. Tall and lean—not skinny, but not bulky either.

As he approached, she swore she saw a softening of his hard mouth, as if he almost remembered how to smile. She bet he had a nice smile but that softness vanished, leaving only the stark mask of his face.

Somehow she had to get up her courage to talk to him. "I didn't get a chance to thank you last night. You disappeared into the rain before I could."

He took the hat she offered, looking at it, then at the ground. At anything but her. "Just doing what anyone would do."

"No, that's not true." Standing here went against every life lesson she'd learned, but somehow it felt as if she were doing more than returning the cap, more than thanking him. It felt personal. He couldn't know how hard it was to slip from behind the hard shell she held up to men, and he'd already been gruff to her.

But she kept going. It was the right thing to do.

"A lot of people hate to get involved. My

sister had our day's earnings on her, and if there had been trouble, well, we could have lost more than that. It's heartening to know there are men like you in this world. I just wanted to thank—"

"C'mon, lady, you can't be real." He hardened before her eyes, his mouth twisting, his dark eyes flashing black. He grabbed the cap by the bill and lopped it onto his head. Gave it a yank to secure it in place. "I don't want your thanks. I don't need your thanks. Whatever it is you're thinking you can get from me, forget it."

Amy's jaw dropped. His fierceness shocked her. She reeled as if he'd slapped her, and she couldn't think, couldn't move. She could only stare after him as he about-faced and climbed into his truck.

Without a look back, he gunned the engine and drove off with a roar, leaving her in his dust.

Chapter Four

⌒

What a perfectly horrible man! She was still fuming many hours later as she trudged across the school's back field that had been divided into over a dozen peewee soccer zones. Kids were everywhere, with their parents and siblings streaming from the jammed parking lot. She'd left her reliable sedan parked beside the city street because she knew there was no way she'd find a spot close coming so late.

Half of the games were in progress. Kids played in groups of six, their primary-colored shirts and shorts bright in the noon sun. Whistles shrieked over the sounds of coaches' orders rising above the children's voices.

A dog barked as he ran from one field to

the other, happily evading the grade schooler who ran after him. "Rufus! Rufus, get back here!"

It was little Allie McKaslin. Her cousin Karen's kid was the same age as her Westin. She wore the red-and-white uniform of the team the diner sponsored. With her fine blond hair flying, she managed to snatch the leash, halting the big golden retriever. Apparently, the match hadn't started yet.

"Hey, Allie!" Amy called to the little girl, circling around a game in progress, hurrying past the orange cones serving as goal posts. "Where's the rest of your team?"

"Oh, hi, Amy!" The blond little sweetheart laughed as the dog gave her a lick across her face. "It's way, way over there."

"Want to come over with me?"

"Yeah!"

Girl and dog fell in beside her, the dog swinging at the end of the leash trying to sniff everything and Allie hopping along as if she were playing hopscotch.

All that energy. Amy sure could use some of that right now. The ice chest was unbelievably heavy—hadn't she vowed last week not to bring so much stuff? She glanced at the spectators lined up a few feet beyond the foul lines. She saw familiar faces, but it took her a while to spot her family.

Once she did, it was hard to believe anyone could miss the crowd of McKaslins. Her sisters and cousins were settled into folding canvas chairs, talking, laughing and shouting encouragement at the soccer players as they warmed up. Vaguely she was aware of Allie handing the dog's leash to someone else and a chorus of greetings, but her gaze shot straight to her son.

Her little Westin looked handsome in his red shirt and matching shorts and sleek dark suntan. He'd been watching for her, as always, and gave her a quick wave. She sent one back his way, waggling her fingers and losing her grip on the corner of the cooler.

"Whew, I got that just in time." Rachel came to the rescue, rising smoothly from the nearby chair, and they lowered the chest in unison. "It weighs a ton. What did you put in there? Anything good?"

"Open it and see."

She heard the short blast of the coach's whistle, one of the high-school girls on the local team, and looked up just in time to see

Westin charge the ball. He stumbled but managed to recover. He drew back his foot and sent the ball limping through the orange cones.

Amy whistled. Rachel shouted. The extended family clapped and hooted. Amy's heart melted as her little boy held up his fists in victory.

Linna, the coach, stopped it with the ball of her foot. "All right, Westin! Good job."

Amy warmed inside as Westin beamed. They'd worked so hard this past week on that kick. She was so proud of him. He looked more confident as he shot her a winning smile before joining the other children in line, waiting their turns with the ball.

"Wow, he's gotten that kick down good." Rachel snapped open the cooler. "What do you have in here—ooh, my very favorite. You shouldn't have."

"I couldn't resist." It was pleasure to watch the happiness light her sister's face as she dried off the strawberry soda can on her sweatshirt and popped the top. She owed Rachel more than she could ever repay, and whatever she could do to make her sister smile made her happy, too.

Cousin Karen came over, her six-month-old daughter on her hip. She held out a plastic container. "Thought I'd make a trade for one of those sodas."

"Not your grandma's famous cookies?"

"Two whole dozen. I was making a batch for us last night and I couldn't resist doubling it. Did you want me to take Westin after the game, or is Rachel going to?"

"Rachel said something about spoiling him this afternoon. I know, it's hard to believe." They both glanced at Rachel, who was sipping her soda, seated in her chair, baseball cap shading her face as she rooted for every kid who kicked the ball.

"Thanks, though. How's little Autumn doing?" She couldn't resist stroking the baby's rose-petal-soft cheek.

The baby girl gurgled and gave a wide grin.

Amy's heart split wide open. "Oh, she's a sweetie."

"She is, most of the time." With a wink, Karen nuzzled her beloved daughter. "Do you want to hold her?"

"You know I do." Amy handed the cookie container to Rachel, who let out a squeal of delight, and took the little girl in her arms. She stopped to watch as Allie, Karen's oldest daughter, boldly gave a mighty kick at the soccer ball…and missed.

She looked so cute that it was hard not to laugh, and the spectators did their best to hide their chuckles and sound encouraging instead. Allie got a second chance—this was the warm-up, after all—and managed to bump her toe against the ball and it hopped forward a few inches.

Amy, along with Karen and the rest of the crowd cheered as if Allie'd made the winning goal.

She felt a tug on her hair—Baby Autumn had a handful wrapped and gave a joyful gurgle. "You want all the attention, do you, darling?"

"Oh, don't hog the baby!" Rachel set her soda can in the holder in the chair's arm, brushed chocolate cookie crumbs off the front of her sweatshirt and held out her hands. "It's my turn."

Gently Amy disentangled her hair from Autumn's dimpled fist and handed over the baby. Rachel immediately started cooing.

Whistles blasted—the game was about to

start. Westin's cheeks were pink with delight as he crouched into the huddle.

"Hey, where's Paige?" Another cousin—Michelle—knelt down between the chairs. "Oh, wait, I know, she's chaperoning the youth group. Isn't she supposed to be back today?"

"Not today! Don't scare us like that!" Rachel teased. "She's going to interrogate me about the books I kept while she was gone, and I'm not very good with the books. I have until tomorrow, the day of doom, when she gets ahold of the ledger."

"I brought those terrible nacho chips, they were on sale in the Shop Mart, and I got three bags for the greater good of everyone else. So please, eat them before I do." She dropped a bright red bag on Amy's lap.

"Okay, but who's going to rescue *me* from these chips?"

"I will." Rachel was all too quick to snatch the bag and yank it open, making them all laugh.

Michelle gave Amy's hair a quick inspection. "Don't you go putting off your hair appointment again. Your highlights are growing out. Don't argue, just come anyway. Well, I'd better get back to my little ones."

After Michelle hurried back to her toddlers and baby, Amy and Rachel crunched chips, sipped on cool sodas and watched as the game started. The teenage girls were trying to direct the little kids, who were doing their best, but ran the wrong way, missed the ball, kicked to the wrong team and forgot what to do when the ball came to them.

"This is so funny," Rachel said as she grabbed her camera and began taking snapshots in quick succession.

Her sister's laughter warmed her through, and Westin's squeal of happiness as he kicked another goal uplifted her even more. The crowd cheered, and Amy soaked it up.

This was why she was so grateful every day. She had the warm Montana sun on her face and the loving acceptance of her family and friends surrounding her. Not to mention her little boy grinning from ear to ear as he ran a victory lap, forgetting to go back to the game, which went on without him.

"Oh, I've got that recorded." Cousin Kendra came over with her handheld DVD video recorder. "I'll make a copy for you. He's too cute."

A shadow moved at the corner of Amy's

eye, drawing her attention to the far edge of the school yard, beyond the tall chain-link fencing to the road out of town.

She recognized the man inside the blue pickup, which was creeping along in obedience to the school zone speed limit. She was surprised he'd stayed in town this long. The loner didn't look right or left, just kept a slow steady speed down the tree-lined lane and kept on going until he was out of sight.

His sadness clung to her as if it had somehow seeped through her skin and settled in her bones. She decided Jodi, the morning-shift waitress, was right. He was the saddest man she'd ever seen. It made it hard to stay angry with him, because he was alone.

And she was not.

The crowd around her came to life, yelling this time for little Allie, who kicked and missed a perfect goal shot. Westin came running to fend off a little boy in a blue uniform, giving her the chance to try again. Everyone leapt out of the chairs and onto their feet, shouting encouragement.

Amy was on her feet cheering, too, as the goal was made, but she couldn't see for the tears in her eyes. Tears that hurt as they fell, not from pain but from gratitude. She never questioned that God was good, look how gracious He had been to her when she had made so many mistakes.

And the loner…

Please watch over him, Father, she prayed, because she knew how bitter loneliness could make someone. And how bleak hopelessness could be.

Heath shifted into fourth gear as the town fell behind him and he accelerated on the two-lane country road. The look on Amy's face had stayed with him the entire time he'd been at the sheriff's office. Even when he and the deputy found out they'd served in the first Desert Storm within twenty miles of one another, *she* had been in the back of his thoughts, and that was saying something.

He couldn't get rid of the dark trembling feeling in his gut, that bad feeling he got whenever he did something he regretted. And what he'd said to the blond-haired woman who'd been decent enough to return his hat, who was simply a nice person—

He couldn't get past it. He'd been mean to her when she'd done nothing to deserve it.

It wasn't like him to behave like that. He never should have acted that way. He'd just been...wrong. Sure, there were a dozen excuses as to why he'd done it, but really, he didn't want to get close to a woman again. In any way, shape or form. There were plenty of reasons, but what did it matter, in the end? Excuses didn't erase the way he'd intentionally pushed her away.

"Some of the nicest people you'll ever meet, the McKaslins," the deputy had told him after he'd filled out a report on last night's troublemakers. "When I first came to town to interview for this job, I'd stopped afterward for a bite to eat at the diner. It was after the lunch rush, and Amy was alone in the place."

"Is it her restaurant?"

"The family's. Those women work hard, I tell you, and they make some of the best meals around. Anyway, after Amy grilled up my burger and gave me a whole batch of fries, she whipped up the best shake I've had anywhere."

When Frank had gotten up to refill the coffee cups, it would have been a good time to have left. But for some reason Heath hadn't made a break for the door. He'd sat there, torn between wanting out and wanting to stay and hear more.

The deputy was more than happy to keep talking. "Amy found out I was the new deputy and offered me the apartment upstairs, it was vacant at the time, to stay in while I looked for a place in town. That was real nice, don't you think?"

"Sure." Built-in business, Heath had thought. Those McKaslin sisters were smart. It went to figure that Frank would buy most if not all of his meals at the diner if he was living above it.

"Empty real estate is pretty scarce around here, even apartments, and so I jumped on her offer. But Amy and her sisters wouldn't take a penny of rent, no sir. They kept me fed and happy, even fed my brothers when they came to help me move in. I tell you, I've never met a nicer family. Generous. Kind. They're the kind of folks who don't think about getting more than they give. With the things I've seen in my life, it's reassuring to know there are still honest-to-God good people in this world."

Yeah, the deputy's words kept replaying in

his head like a CD stuck on repeat. Words that grated against his conscience with every mile that passed.

Good people. Generous and kind. Those words hurt him in a way nothing had in a very long time. Longer than he wanted to count or to think about. For about as long as he'd turned his back on his old life. Nothing could hurt like the pain he left behind, but the prick of his conscience just kept going on and on.

Maybe it was the soft green of the rolling countryside, where new crops grew in endless fields on either side of the narrow country road. It was idyllic, it truly was. Like something on television with a filter over the camera lens to make the greens brighter and the blues deeper, to make life more vivid and beautiful than it could ever be in reality.

Tidy driveways veered off the main road, about a quarter of a mile or more apart, where mailboxes stood bearing the family name, some in the shapes of barns or decorated to look like a duck. The graveled driveways wound through the green fields and the country homes seemed to smile, although it was only the reflection of the sunlight on the front windows.

He saw everything from trailer homes to lavish houses. It was all so neat and quaint, with horses grazing in white-fenced pastures and now and then a farmer riding a tractor along the fence line. Irrigation tossed water into the wind, and thousands of tiny rainbows glittered midair in the spray.

The beauty surrounding him made him feel keenly what he'd become inside—ugly and bitter.

Had he become so hard and callous that he could no longer recognize good when he saw it? He remembered the look on the waitress's face. The stunned shock and the sudden hurt as if he'd reached out and slapped her—not that he would ever hit a woman.

But that's how much harm his panicked words had done.

C'mon, lady, you can't be real. Whatever it is you're thinking you can get from me, forget it.

Yeah, he could hear how it would have sounded to her. He'd become so bitter, it felt as if it was all he was. Nothing but disillusionment and pain, and he was ashamed of himself. Ashamed. He wasn't a bad man. He didn't go around hurting people.

So why had he said that to her?

Because he'd stopped believing in good, in kindness, long ago. It was easier than the truth he could not bear to face. It was easier than trying to understand why God had taken so much from him. And why—

Black pain clamped so tight on his heart, he gasped. Air caught in his throat. He'd swear he was having a heart attack, but he knew better. It was a different kind of pain in his heart. A different kind of damage.

The road stretched ahead of him, rolling and ribboning up the gentle rises and falling out of sight in the slow dips. Then it rose again in the distance, like a thin black thread lying along the endless green. The road could carry him far away, past those mountains rising up thousands of feet, the rugged, bare-faced granite and white glacier caps holding up the vivid blue bowl of the sky.

Yeah, he could keep going on this road, keeping on just the way he was. Adding this stain on his soul to go along with the emptiness in there. He could drive east and once he had those mountains behind him, he could forget this place ever existed and with it the wrong he'd done. He *could* go on.

But he didn't want to be the kind of man who did. He might have lost everything on a rainy night over two years ago. That didn't mean he had to grow into the kind of man who went around causing harm.

No, Lord knew there were enough of those kinds of people on this earth already.

Was he going to be one of them? Suddenly he saw how it worked: One mistake after another, one harm caused after another, until it was a way of life.

So he stopped in the middle of the road. With the windows down, sweet fragrant air breezed into the cab. As it bathed his face and tickled his hair, he debated. Then he checked for traffic—not that there was a vehicle in sight in either direction. And, with no one but God to witness it, he pulled a U-turn and headed back the way he came. Not so bitter a man, after all.

Not so lost.

The diner was jammed. Amy gave thanks for the warm sunny day because they could use the tables set out on the brick patio at the side of the building. Without them, they'd be turning business away. As it was, they were almost out of those tables, too.

As Jodi seated another soccer family, Amy filled orders as fast as the grill would cook them. She was glad the twins—young though they were—had shown up early to help with some of the prep work.

"Westin is like the coolest kid ever!" Brandilyn—or was it Brianna?—grabbed the order for table three and, instead of hurrying, stopped, cracked her gum and gave a high-wattage smile. "I can't wait until I get to be a mom. Not that I'm in a hurry, 'cuz I hope I can get into college first."

It was Brandilyn because Brianna sidled up to actually take the plates from the warming lights. Amy could clearly see the name badge on her collar.

Equally as blond and cute and full of teenage charm, Brianna cracked her gum, too. "Like, college is a year away. We're supposed to be waitresses, Brand. So, like, waitress, okay?"

"Oh, right!" With a swing of her head, which sent her ponytail flopping, Brandilyn grabbed the last plate and followed her twin down the aisle.

"We were never like that when we were their age," Jodi commented as she brought in a bin of dirties and dumped them on the counter. "Right?"

"Right. We never giggled. Never used words like *cool*." Amy laughed as she unloaded small glass plates of house salad from the refrigerator and uncovered them. "Is it me, or does it seem like a century since we were that young?"

"For me, two centuries at least." Jodi hadn't had the easiest life, either, but she managed to smile. "Those two are the cutest things. I adore 'em, except they make me feel about twelve hundred years old."

"Oh, wait until they pull you aside for their senior life class assignment." Amy trayed the plates and left Jodi to finish them as the fryer beeped. She had fries to rescue.

"I'm afraid to ask," Jodi said as she spooned out the creamy salad dressings.

"They wanted to know what school was like in the 'olden days.'"

"*What?*" A spoon clattered to the floor and rattled to a stop. "The olden days?"

"Sure. I'm practically thirty and, as they said, that's 'like ancient.'" Amy lovingly mimicked the twins' intonation as she set the basket out of the grease and turned to add slices of cheese to half of the frying meat patties. "You gotta love those two."

"Or something!" Jodi was laughing—or maybe crying. Several years older, Jodi was well into her midthirties and, Amy suspected, unappreciative ofbeing called ancient. "I've got a few crow's feet, but goodness! The olden days. Did they really say that?"

"Honest and truly. I wish I could say they meant to be insulting, but they said it as cheerful as could be. Just wait." Amy reached with the tongs to rescue the buns from the browning rack—but missed. Her fingers froze in midair, woefully short of the metal tongs.

The screen door behind her squeaked. Turning, she saw a tall, broad-shouldered man fill the doorway.

Her loner was back, and he didn't look happy. "Can I come in?"

"We're busy."

"I need to talk to you."

"I'm busy."

Heath knew that look and what it meant when it was on a woman's face. He was in the doghouse, no doubt about that. His hand was raised in a loose fist to knock on the metal door frame, but since he'd already been spotted, he lowered his hand. He tried to gather up his pride and his troubled conscience.

The other waitress took one look at him, grabbed her tray of salads and disappeared through the swinging doors, leaving him alone with Amy McKaslin, who turned her back on him to whisk two burgers from the grill with a neat jab of the big metal spatula. She deposited them on well-dressed bottom buns, added bacon to one and sauce and pineapple rings to the other and, finishing with the top bun, loaded them onto plates.

He knew the look of hard, honest work. His conscience smote him even harder as, with her back to him, she kept on working. Her golden-blond ponytail bounced in rhythm with her movements, the curling end brushing at the collar of her T-shirt. It was a vulnerable thing, seeing the soft creamy skin and the visible bumps of her vertebrae. She was small-boned and fragile, and yet she worked with a strong capability that said she was made of steel, too.

He'd hurt her more than he'd realized, and he felt sick about it. He could see that in the rigid way she kept her back to him as she worked. Flipping strips of bacon, stirring sautéing onions, changing gloves to drop fresh oversized buns onto the rack to warm.

"Maybe you could spare a minute?"

She didn't so much as flinch. "I don't really have a minute to spare."

"I can see you're in the middle of a lunch crowd."

She arched her brow, her face a set mask as she rushed by to lift a bin of sliced tomatoes from the industrial refrigerator. Okay, she wasn't going to make this easy for him, he understood it. He respected her for it, too. She was a nice person, but she wasn't a pushover. He liked women with a bit of grit to them.

So he tried again. "I just wanted to apologize. I'll only take, say, thirty seconds of your time."

"Believe me, if you want to apologize properly, it's going to take a lot more than thirty seconds." She kept her back to him, swapping gloves again, dressing toasted buns with relish and mayonnaise, adding lettuce and tomato.

She didn't seem quite as angry. Maybe that

was a good sign. He gave his cap's bill a tug as he thought. He wasn't sure what to say other than that he'd behaved like a donkey's behind. Without reason. "Can I come in? Or are you going to make me stand here and grovel for forgiveness from ten feet away?"

"Are you going to grovel?"

He thought he heard a smiling sound in her voice, but he couldn't be sure. "How would you like it? On my knees? Prostrate on the floor? Maybe wearing sack cloth and covered with boils?"

"Boils? I'd like to see you suffer, but there are health codes to uphold. I guess I'll have to settle for prostrate on the floor. Would you like a towel? The tile's clean but it's the old-fashioned kind and it's cold to lie on."

"Well, if you want me to suffer…" He didn't finish the sentence, and he liked that she turned from her work, a hint of a smile tugging at the curving corners of her soft mouth.

"I do want you to suffer," she confessed, but the questioning tilt of her deep-blue eyes said differently.

She was studying him, as if measuring his intentions, not in a harsh way but in a way that made him feel as if he had a chance of measuring up. But why should he care about that? All he needed to do was ease his conscience, apologize and move on.

He had places to go. A job to find. A past to keep forever buried.

"Come in. It's not locked." She went back to work, flipping the burgers, dumping a huge pile of freshly cut potatoes into the French-fry basket, lifting another out of the golden oil full of crisp, hand-battered onion rings.

He turned the screen-door handle and the hinges rasped as he stepped inside. Could use some grease, he thought, looking around. The white tile floor was probably original, most likely put in sometime in the sixties. The kitchen was small and simple, but clean. Chrome shined. The countertops were a perfect white. The appliances up to date.

He didn't know what made him open his mouth or where the words came from. He surprised himself when he heard his voice say, "Want some help?"

She dropped her spatula. Spun on her heel. Surveyed him up and down with her intelligent eyes. "Do you have a food handler's card?"

"Got one a while back. It's still current."

"Okay, then. You can seat folks. Gather up the empties. Bus. Can you do that?" It wasn't a question the way she said it; it was more of a challenge. As if she wanted to see if he could measure up to her standards.

He hadn't had a challenge in a long while. Not that he was worried—he liked to work hard. She pointed at the sink and he washed up, letting the hot water scald his skin. He didn't know what whim he was following, but whatever it was, it had to be a good one. His conscience wasn't bugging him. His stomach was calm. He felt as if he was finally doing something right as he grabbed an empty dishpan and shouldered through the swinging doors.

Out of the corner of his peripheral vision, he saw Amy watching him in surprise before the doors swung closed, stealing her from his sight. He didn't know why, but he felt a sense of rightness click into place like a key in a lock, and it was as if a door opened. In his old life, he would have chalked it up to Providence, but he'd long since stopped looking— or wanting—God's hand in his life.

But now he just saw it as a fortunate occurrence. That's all, not Providence. He spotted a family leaving one of the booths. The father took the wiggling toddler from his wife, who looked kind but a little harried, as she encouraged her older two sons—both wearing different colored soccer uniforms—to stop goofing around on their way down the aisle.

Heath looked away and froze his feelings so he felt nothing at all. He was just a man staring out the window, working in a diner, more interested in the few cars crawling by looking for parking. The family passed by on their way to the cash register up front.

Only then did he plop the bin on the seat and start clearing.

Chapter Five

Amy flipped the double patties on the garnished bottom bun, added hot sauce, jalapeños and hot peppers, and heaped fries on the last plate on the last order of the Saturday lunch rush. Through the hand-off window she could see the last of the families were waiting for Jodi to ring up their meals.

Amy turned to begin clean-up and then halted in midstep. What was she thinking? She *wasn't* thinking, that was the problem. Her thoughts had been scattered like dust in the wind and she couldn't seem to get them focused. Not since the loner had returned. He was a good worker—she had to give him that. Through the swinging doors she could just see the top of his head as he wiped down the outside tables.

She still didn't know if she had completely forgiven him for being so rude to her, and that was wrong. It was her faith to forgive. He'd offered her a sincere apology and she had accepted it. But deep down his harsh demeanor grated. See, it was good never to trust men. Whether they meant to or not, they caused pain.

She'd had enough pain in her life and certainly wasn't about to look for more. So, why did she keep wondering about him? Why had he come back? Why was he helping out? Where was he going, that he had time to spare instead of rushing off to wherever it was that he'd been heading?

The swinging doors burst open—it was one of the twins. Tall and willowy and colt-like in the way of teenagers, and radiating pure energy.

Brianna, a touch theatrical, gave a deep meaningful sigh. "I'm, like, totally starving. I'd give anything for, like, a totally loaded chiliburger. Oh, and can I have lots and lots of fries? I burned off, like, an awesome amount of calories."

Maybe the twins were terrible behind the cash register, but they were fun. Amy bit her lip to keep from laughing and got to work. Knowing Brandilyn would be waltzing in any second with the exact same request, she set two buns on to toast while she dished out two scoops of the chili stocked in the fridge, put them in a bowl and placed it in the microwave to warm.

Brianna, in the middle of counting up tip money, stopped to add, "Ooh, and, like, cheese, too." Then she looked down at the big stack of ones, rolled her eyes, huffed out another sigh and started counting all over again.

She loved the twins, but really, she was glad she'd never have to be a teenager again. She wouldn't go back for anything. Sometimes it was painful to look at the girls and remember when she'd been that age—and far too rebellious. She'd been the top student in her class all through high school, but she'd never made it through her senior year.

And the years after that…no, she wasn't interested in looking back at that time. It was better to act as if she'd been able to erase it from her memory, like words from a blackboard, so that it was as clean as if it had never been.

"Here's your cut." Brianna slapped a stack of ones on the counter. "Oh, and isn't Heath totally awesome? Are you, like, gonna hire him for keeps?"

Heath? So that was his name. She resisted the urge to peer through the doors—she could hear the faint clink and clank of dishes as he bussed. She deliberately kept her voice low and even. "He offered to pitch in and help us out for this shift. I don't know what his plans are."

"You should make him take the cook job. Well, only if he can cook, you know? 'Cause, like—"

Brandilyn burst through the doors, ready to finish her twin's sentence. "He'd be cool to have around. He's this awesome mysterious kind of guy. Like from movies and stuff. You know he's a good guy, but he's so totally distant and almost scary."

"But nice," Brianna added. "Definitely nice."

"Yeah." They nodded together, both blond heads and ponytails bouncing. "Don't you think he's nice?"

Amy flipped the meat patties, shaking her

head. There they were again, trying to find her a husband. And, to use their words—as if!

She did her best to hide a smile, because she didn't want to encourage them. "I'm just interested in hiring a cook. You girls go get your sodas. Your burgers are ready."

"Cool!" they said, spun on their heels and blew through the kitchen, leaving her alone.

As she dressed the buns and built the sandwiches, she let her mind wander over the possibilities. Heath. The name suited him and she liked it.

"So, are you going to tell me about the job?"

Startled, her hand flew to her throat. Trembling, she tried to catch her breath. He stood there, legs apart and braced, dressed in black jeans and T-shirt, his dark gaze fixed on her. He reminded her of a lone wolf, lean and sizable and fierce looking. She didn't feel in danger around him, but she didn't feel exactly safe either.

"You scared me. I didn't hear you there."

"Sorry."

He didn't look sorry. And yet she thought she heard a sense of humor warming that one word.

He looked less imposing as the hint of a grin curved the far corner of his mouth. "Next time I'll stomp my feet and bang hard on the door so you can hear me coming."

"Great idea. Maybe you could rattle some pots."

"I'll try."

The grin spread across his hard-shaped lips until it softened his chiseled features.

It was infectious, and she couldn't help smiling in return. That was dangerous, no doubt about it. She'd learned the hard way men can't be trusted. Of course, there were a few shining exceptions in the world like Pastor Bill and Uncle Pete and her brother, but this dark loner with his guarded stance and his discontent definitely looked like trouble.

He looked like the kind of man who, no matter how good, was always moving on. The kind who left devastation in his wake.

"I don't think you're right for the position." She hated being so terse, but it was the truth. Judging by the way he kept staring at the door, he was already as good as gone. "There's no way I want to train someone who's got to be somewhere else by the end of the week. Sorry."

"Who said I had someplace else to be?"

"Well, you were driving through town, remember? I assume you had a destination in mind."

"I've got nothing important ahead of me."

It was the way he said it—as if it was no big deal, a take it or leave it kind of a way. Amy wasn't fooled. In the silence that stretched between them, as she set the two plates oozing with big juicy sandwiches and mountains of fries under the warmer, she felt the seconds lengthen and stretch.

And she saw the edges of his shoes, scuffed and worn and patched with duct tape and shoe polish over the tape to disguise it. He'd done a good job, but she recognized the same technique she used on her shoes when times were lean.

I've never seen a sadder-looking man. People got all kinds of heartaches, we both know that, but it just sort of clung to him like an aftershave or something. Just so much sadness. Jodi's words came back to her as bold as a touch from heaven above, and Amy shivered down deep, not from the cold but from the simple truth that he was in need.

She knew exactly how that felt. "That

chiliburger smells good. Would you like to have one with me? And don't get all worked up when I tell you it's free. You work a shift, you get a free meal. It isn't charity, it's our policy."

He had the grace to blush a little. "I was a jerk, and I'm sorry for it. The truth is, I don't like charity. I can make my own way through life."

"Sure, but we all need a little help from time to time. Even us strong stoic types."

Her words rubbed him wrong, and if her tone had been less friendly and less matter-of-fact, it would have set him off again. He still had his pride—he'd about lost everything else.

But Amy was already slapping beef patties on the grill, and the truth was, he'd worked in enough restaurants to know a free meal with a work shift was policy in a lot of places. It had nothing to do with her thinking he needed charity.

Besides, he had no right getting mad at her. She ran a good business. She treated her waitstaff well—he'd have to be blind not to see it. And she looked exhausted. While she came across as energetic and competent, he could see the telltale signs of the tiredness she was covering up. The slight droop of her shoulders. The pale tint to her face. The dark smudges that bruised the delicate skin beneath her eyes.

He respected anyone who worked so hard. Maybe it was simple good luck that he'd come back. A job? Here? He thought it over as he looked around for something needing done—the garbage bin was full—and he tied off the sack, hefted it out of the plastic container and blew through the screen door.

Stay here? Why not? The warm sunshine seemed to embrace him and the gentle breeze felt like a caress against his forehead. The familiar urban smell of sun-warmed blacktop was softened by the scent of ripening grasses from the fields visible at the end of the long block, where town ended and the country began. The scent of fresh lilacs reminded him of his grandmother's house as he hefted the sack into the Dumpster.

Feeling lighter somehow, he gazed up at the small second story, which was visible from the back of the building. He hadn't noticed it before. A row of windows sparkled and glinted in the light, and he spotted a row of stairs rising along the far side of the building. The deputy had mentioned an apartment. Was anyone living there now? There was no sign that someone was.

"Hey, quite an afternoon, ain't it?" The grizzled clerk from the hotel crossed the alley. Nearly bald, what little hair he had was white as snow, and he walked with a stoop and a limp. He was a lean man, nearly skin and bones, but he had spryness to his step. "You workin' for the girls?"

"Thinking about it."

"You couldn't find nicer people. It's heartening how those girls have worked to make a go of this. They could use some help after that cook they hired just ran off. Got a notion to see North Dakota and left them shorthanded. You a good cook?"

"I'm passable."

"Good. Okay, then. See ya around."

Heath chuckled, watching the man limping down the alley to where the sidewalk led around the corner of the building.

"If you pass Joe's muster, I guess you've got yourself a job."

It was Amy, nothing more than a shadow behind the mesh of the screen door. She was hard to see as she reached for the door, and then the squeaking hinges gave way to the flare of sunlight. Her hair gleamed like polished gold, her red T-shirt glowed like a ruby and her white flowered apron ruffled in the breeze. She smiled, holding the door open for him.

If that wasn't a sign he ought to stay, then he didn't know what was. He was down on his luck, had been for a long while, but that didn't mean he was without luck. It was amazing how fate stepped in at the last moment with a job or something to help him get by. He used to chalk it up to the Lord, when he'd been naive, when he'd believed there was good in the world and someone wise and compassionate in charge of the universe.

He knew better now, but he did long for those simpler times. Simpler because he'd had faith, because the world had been friendlier and less cold when he'd truly believed. Life since had been complicated and everything seemed a little nicer here, in this small town where people smiled as they went about their business.

Yeah, this might be a real nice place to stay for a while.

He caught the edge of the screen door. Her smile fading, she turned away from him and moved farther into the kitchen. Moving easily, she handed him a platter. She'd given him an enormous helping, but he decided not to complain or take it the wrong way.

He'd work the rest of the day, that would make things a little more even. "I can see you need help around here. Your cook took off on you, right? And now you think I might do the same."

"I need help, don't get me wrong. I'd love to hire someone to deal with the grill—cooking isn't my favorite thing, not that I'm complaining. It's just…how long would you be interested in staying?"

"So, you meant what you said. You'll hire me?"

"Something like that. You didn't answer my question." She pushed through the doors and led the way.

"Oh, hire him, Amy!" One of the teenage waitresses called across the dining room, where she sat near the front door with her identical sister.

"Yeah, you've been working here totally too long every day. That's not good for you.

You need time for exercise and rest and stuff."

Amy slid her plate on the edge of a small table. A table for two, and Heath had the distinct impression that she didn't want him eating with her or cooking in her kitchen.

"Sit down, get comfortable, help yourself to a soda." She gestured to the empty tables, leaving it clear. She hadn't forgotten how he'd treated her. And he didn't blame her, because forgiving was one thing, but she clearly was a woman who didn't trust easily.

I'm the same way, he thought with relief. He chose a booth near the window, so he could look out while he ate. His stomach growled, and his mouth watered. The scent of the burger alone was incredible. Amy had made him a big sandwich. It took both hands to hold it and it was all he could do to take a bite. Cheese dripped, chili oozed and the beef tasted good—fresh, not like it had been overprocessed and frozen and shipped across a continent. He'd bet the supplier was local. She probably bought straight from the local butcher.

It was the tastiest food he'd had in a long time.

He turned his attention out the window,

where a lazy Saturday afternoon shone like a dream. He had the feeling the town hadn't changed much in fifty years. A few cars ambled past. A pair of boys raced by on their bikes. Beyond the park and railroad tracks he spotted black-and-white cows grazing in a field, and the sharp blast of a horn said the train would be coming through at any moment.

He'd been a boy the last time he'd sat and really watched a train, and he felt the thrill of anticipation as the horn tooted, announcing its imminent arrival. The earth would rumble, or at the very least it would seem that way if he were close enough, as the huge black engine charged into sight. Heath counted three engines hitched together, capably drawing the long snake of the freight cars behind. His grandfather had loved trains. He'd given Heath a real Lionel railroad set—a collector's item now, but who knew what had become of it?

If Granddad were here, he'd have liked this place. He would have said no town could be half bad if it had a train going through it. His grandfather had always longed to travel, and maybe that was what trains always meant to him, but he'd been a farmer with his feet rooted firmly in Texas soil.

This cozy rural town reminded Heath of his summer trips to stay with his grandparents. Not the terrain—there was no mistaking Montana with her mountains and lush rolling valleys for the dry brown flat expanse of central Iowa. But this place, too, was a one-street town, where folks went just a little bit slower, were kinder, and knew their neighbors. In that way, it felt familiar—not like home, no, never that, but a good place to stay for a while.

The phone rang somewhere up near the cash register. Down the aisle, Amy hopped up, chewing on a long French fry, and jogged to catch it. She told the twins to relax as she skirted the counter, reached down and popped up with a handheld receiver. She brightened like creek water when sunlight hits it and turned her back, her voice a warm melody.

He ate everything on his plate—he was hungrier than he'd thought. He polished off a tall glass of frothy root beer and considered. The waitresses had given him a fair cut of the tips. He had cash enough, added with what he'd had in his wallet, to see him through the rest of the week or so, if he was careful. He wasn't in a bad position, not bad at all.

There was no reason to accept Amy's job offer. This place, while it reminded him of better times in his life, had too many families. Too many friendly people. He'd leave, it was the best decision.

Still, it was with regret that he pushed out of the chair and took his plate back to the kitchen. He would have liked working here.

Amy shouldered through the doors and took his plate from him before he could add it to the stack Jodi, the other waitress, was rinsing.

"Hey, where are you going?" Amy looked friendly enough, he decided, but there was a hard set to her face. She slipped a key into his palm.

He stared at it, confused. "A key? What for?"

"To the room upstairs. I thought—I mean Rachel and I thought—that you might want to stay there. You did want the job, right?"

Amy watched, heart racing, trepidation rushing through her bloodstream. Heath studied the plain, ordinary key, as if she'd offered him a handful of radioactive waste.

Maybe he thought this was charity, too, since he was touchy on the subject. "The apartment can be part of your pay, if you want it. It isn't much, but it's clean and furnished. Why don't you go take a look at it and decide it you want to stay there, even just for the night instead of in another motel room."

"You seem pretty sure of this. You were worried about me running off and leaving you shorthanded."

"It's still a concern of mine, but Rachel has faith in you. She said she liked the cut of your character, helping us out the way you did last night, and stepping in today when others wouldn't have. Besides, she also pointed out that we're shorthanded now, that's the problem. We'll solve it by hiring you. Do we have a deal?"

He looked around, took his time before he answered. "I know I made a donkey's behind of myself when we first met, and I'm sorry for the way I acted. I won't do it again. If you can put the way I treated you behind us, then I'd like to work here."

Should she be surprised that he'd apologized again? She didn't have a lot of experience with an honest apology from a man—well, those from her brother didn't count, and brothers were brothers. She knew she could trust him. But what about Heath—could she trust him?

She studied him, trying to see more than what he appeared to be. With the slant of the sun through the door, burnishing his powerful frame with vivid light, he was startling. He was a big man—not bulky with thick muscles, but not lean either. There was a latent power that seemed to burn in him, leashed and waiting.

His hair wasn't black, as it had appeared last night in the dark, but a rich bitter-chocolate-brown. His high forehead and strong cheekbones were not harsh, but intelligent and well-defined. Although he was handsome, his features were set in an unmistakable expression that said, "Keep away." He was a private man and a self-sufficient one.

"I can put it behind us." Amy understood, too, having pride. "Go check out the room. Let one of us know if you need anything, all right?"

He was already shaking his head, already

pushing through the door. "I don't need anything. When did you want me to start?"

"How about you come in around four? Rachel's in the kitchen tonight, and she'll walk you through the prep and train you on the grill. Is that all right?"

"Yep." His mouth compressed into a tight thin line. Serious, sincere, he met her gaze. The impact of their eyes meeting felt like a jolt of lightning to her soul.

"I don't want you to worry about me," he assured her. "I work hard. I do my best. I don't want to cause anyone any harm or grief. I just want to be left alone."

His words weren't harsh, but they were definite. Don't get too friendly, he was saying.

Well, good, because that was her motto, too. She was close to her family and her friends, but that was it. At least this was something she and the loner agreed on—distance. Maybe he knew, too, it was the only way to keep safe.

"Rachel will be waiting for you at four," she said in agreement.

As if he understood, he gave her a curt nod and disappeared from her sight.

* * *

Heath didn't set his hopes high as he fit the key into the decades-old knob. From the outside, he wasn't expecting the place to be much at all. He turned the key until the lock released. No dead bolt, he noticed. Then again, there probably wasn't much crime in a town like this.

The door swung open, giving in to gravity when Heath released the knob and it shuddered to a stop against the wall. He saw only dim shadows, the outline of lemony light ebbing around the pull-down blinds at the windows and noticed the mildew and dust odor of a room long unused.

He decided to leave the door open. Maybe some fresh air would improve the place. It was a good thing he'd known not to expect too much. There'd been a time in his life when he'd gotten so much, he came to take it for granted. His old self, the man he used to be, would have been disappointed for sure over this room where the floorboards beneath his feet groaned and creaked.

He yanked the first blind and it slipped out of his fingers, rolling up with a bang. Bright afternoon light filtered through the screened wood-framed window. Since he wanted fresh air, he tried to open it, but it was stuck. The old paint had gotten damp and tacky. He used a little muscle and the wooden frame began to give. Sunshine seemed to welcome him as he let the fragrant fresh breezes slide past him and into the apartment.

His jaw dropped. Now that he had some light to see better, he couldn't believe his eyes. The front room was bigger than he'd expected. There were the shadows of bricks at the inside wall and the hollow of a fireplace. In front of that sat a living-room set. Two couches and a chair had to be second-hand, because the style was several decades old, but the furniture was clean and the tan upholstery looked like new. He sat on the nearest couch to test it out, and a little cloud of dust rose from the impact of his weight. But what was a little dust?

The cushions were comfortable. There was a small coffee table if he wanted to put up his feet, and, wait…was that a TV remote? He leaned forward and reached out. Yeah, it was. So, were was the TV?

He hit the power button and in front of him, propped on the end table between the couches was a color thirteen-inch screen. An old Western movie flashed the bright pictures of a cattle round-up. The volume was on low, so it was more of a humming drone in the silence.

It wasn't half-bad, he decided as he scoped out the rest of the room. There were two doors in the end wall, the bedroom and bathroom, he figured. And, behind him on the inside wall near the front door was a dark archway that led into what was probably the kitchen. Amy was right, it was clean and comfortable.

Yeah, he could live here. It was a far better place than anywhere he'd stayed in the recent past, which he thought of as his second life. The old life was gone—he was never going back. He couldn't.

His chest began to seize with pain and he carefully wiped even the mention of his past from his mind. It was some time before his chest relaxed and he could breathe normally again—before the silence surrounding him held no traces of memory.

Outside he heard the rasp of tires on the alley's pocked blacktop and the purr of an engine coming closer. A car door snapped shut, echoing. He listened to the tap of a woman's shoes as she hurried to the back kitchen door, directly beneath his open window. The rasp of the screen-door hinges was preceded by a woman calling out.

"Amy! Amy!" It sounded like the other sister's voice, Rachel, the quieter one. "Help, quick! Emergency!"

Adrenaline shot into his veins—it was a call to action. Like a soldier jumping for his weapon, he was on his feet and had his hand on the doorknob. His attention focused so intently that the outside stimulus fell away. He was ready to roll. The sister needed help.

The screen door slammed shut, and her voice went on. "I can't get this ledger thingy to balance and Paige is gonna flip out when she sees it."

A ledger thingy? What was a ledger thingy?

His feet stopped moving, and his hand seized the rail. He realized he was already halfway down the stairs, heart pounding, ready to offer assistance however it should be needed, and there wasn't a real emergency. No one was in danger. No one needed medical attention.

Amy's voice, soft as lark song, answered,

confirming the problem. "Paige is so good at bookkeeping she can't see why everyone doesn't understand it."

"It's like the whole double-posting thing. Why post it twice? I say, add up the numbers from the cash register, subtract it from the checks from the checkbook. But no, there have to be ledgers and accounts payable and amortization schedules."

"Here's a strawberry soda. Sit down, drink it, relax. What time did Linna say the team party would be over?"

"Four."

"Good. We have some time before I have to go. Between the two of us, we ought to be able to figure this out before Paige gets back and blows a circuit."

The sisters sounded less dire as they talked, and now they were laughing easily. He wiped his face with his free hand. He'd walked right into that one, hadn't he? Just like that, he was the old Heath Murdock again. He couldn't stop the past, even in a place like this, hundreds of miles away from home.

He breathed deep, trying to calm down. He took in the surroundings, as if that reminded the deep places in his gray matter that he was in Montana, not Oregon. It was different here. Dry, with a faint haze of dust in the air. And there was the heat of sunshine baking the earth and wildflowers and, farther away, the growing crops. He was no longer walking the old path. He was no longer a doctor ready to offer aid. He couldn't help anyone.

Not anymore.

The sisters were laughing, and Amy was saying, "Why did you put this here? I can't believe you did that."

Rachel chuckled, as if she found her own mistakes the funniest thing. "Yeah, it's wrong, I know, but all I can say is that it sounded like a good thing at the time."

"You are a horrible bookkeeper, Rachel Elizabeth McKaslin."

"I know. It's not news, so when Paige flips out when she sees what I've done with her books, we'll have to both tell her that I told her so. She just wouldn't listen."

"Rachel, you do realize we couldn't pay someone to do this bad a job on purpose."

"Yeah, yeah."

It was a good-natured conversation. Heath didn't mean to listen in, but his feet seemed to have become cemented to the stair beneath his boots. The sisters went on talking, laughing and joking as if they were the best of friends. The deputy's words came back to him. *I've never met a nicer family…. They're the kind of folks who don't think about getting more than they give.* That would sure be a change in his life, he thought, glad that he was going to stay.

He eased down onto the step and let the filtered sunlight from the reaching branches of the trees next door flicker over him. The rustle of leaves, the distant drone of a tractor, the hum of a passing bumblebee, the warm murmur of voices from inside the restaurant…these sounds soothed at the knot of tension he always carried with him.

He felt better than he had in a long, long while. He took a deep breath, letting the clean country air fill him up. A movement through the leaves caught his attention—it was a kindly-looking elderly lady in the next house down the alley a ways. He watched her amble down her porch in a baggy blouse and jeans. The brightly colored garden gloves on her hands and the wide-brimmed hat shading her face told of her intentions.

It was timeless, the picture she made as she knelt at her flowerbeds and bent to work. Maybe weeding, he decided, as she produced one of those metal claws from behind a bush and attacked the ground. A smoke-gray cat sauntered from the shaded porch and curled around the lady, who took off a glove to scratch beneath the feline's chin.

Heath could almost hear the contented purr. Or maybe it was the memory of how his grandmother used to tend her vegetable garden on hands and knees, humming one of her favorite tunes—she was always humming. And he was reminded of how she'd stop to indulge one pet or the other as well as her grandson, whose baseballs often went astray in her flowerbeds.

Those were good memories, and he ached from remembering in a different way. He'd been happy as a boy visiting them. And sitting here remembering made the agony within him ease. Not that he'd ever be happy. No, never that.

The sisters were laughing again, their voices closer, coming from the kitchen by the sound of it. There was some clanging and a bang of cupboards, and then a triumphant, "I found it!"

He wondered what they'd been looking for as the voices faded away to a distant murmur. They must have gone into the dining area.

Quiet filled him. It wasn't happiness, but it was something positive. It felt right that he was here, working for people who were honest and worked hard. And, judging from those roughnecks who'd caused trouble in the lonely diner at night, maybe he could do some good here at the same time. Keep a protective eye on the sisters while he built up his cash funds. It felt right to have the chance to do some good.

It had been a long time since he'd made a difference anywhere.

Chapter Six

"Listen up, bird, you don't want to make a nest on my nice table. Really." The woman's kind words matched the gentle morning.

From his place at the open window at the small table in the kitchen, Heath couldn't see who was talking to birds this early in the morning but he recognized Amy's voice.

He shoved back his chair, neatly missing the refrigerator, and with cup of instant coffee in hand let his curiosity lead him downstairs and around the corner of the building. Maybe she could use some help.

The rumbling rhythm of the train rolling down the steel tracks hid the sound of his footsteps as he rounded a tall hedge of blooming lilacs to the gate through the latticed fence around the outside eating area. Small climbing roses, their buds closed tight, clung to the tall crisscrossed wall, and beyond the green leaves and canes, he could see Amy's profile as she cleaned up the beginning of a bird's nest on one of the patio tables.

The robin hopped from the corner edge of the wall to the top of a chair back. The red-breasted bird looked determined to build her nest. She carried a sturdy tuft of a twig in her beak. The creature did not move, even though Amy was only on the other side of the small metal table.

"I'm sorry, this is my table. You can't build a nest here. Besides, it's not far enough off the ground. There's a cat just across the alley." Amy gathered up the last of the twigs the bird had nestled between the rod of the umbrella and the folded tablecloth yet to be spread out. "This isn't a safe place for your babies anyway."

The robin cocked her head and chirped before lifting her wings as if ready to fight.

He really ought to step in and help Amy

out, but this was a wild bird. Surely it would take off at any minute.

But it didn't. Amy deposited the twigs in a small bag she'd produced from her pile of cushions and tablecloths in disarray on another tabletop.

"I'm really sorry," she explained as she sprayed down the table and wiped it clean. "You have to find somewhere else to make your home."

The bird didn't move.

"Please, shoo." She waved her hand at the robin, who still refused to fly off. "The health department won't like it if you live here. Go. Shoo."

The robin chirped angrily before deciding to retreat to the fence.

"Good. Thank you."

Amy disappeared inside the restaurant, absorbed in her work, moving quick and fast. Her hair was wet from showering and pulled back at her nape. She didn't see him standing on the other side of the gate.

He didn't want to startle her, so he was glad the latch squeaked and the hinges rasped as if they hadn't been opened in years. It was enough noise that she popped her head out the door, spotted him and smiled.

"Good morning. You don't know how happy I am to see you. This is by far our busiest time of the week. Sunday brunch." She was friendly but all business as she led the way to the coffeepot and reached down two cups. "Don't tell me you're drinking that instant stuff someone left in the cupboard about five years ago?"

"It tastes all right."

"No it doesn't." With a smile, she took his cup and gave him a fresh one.

He breathed in the good-quality coffee. "Thanks."

"Rachel said you did great last night and that you've worked a few grills before, from the looks of it. She was very impressed."

"I worked at a truck stop in Dillon for a time. A few other places before that."

That explained it. Amy dumped creamer into her cup, gave thanks and drank deep. The rich taste soothed her. She'd been up late last night, going over the books as she'd promised her sister. Rachel was starting to be much better at bookkeeping than she would admit, but Amy knew she wasn't the most confident person. She'd double-checked her sister's work, just so Rachel would rest easy. Everything was right, squared away and ready for Paige's inspection later this afternoon.

"Do you think you're up to manning the grill? It'll take two to keep up, once church lets out."

"I'm up to it."

"Great." With coffee in hand, she rushed back to the side door, calculating how much she could get done in the time she had left. There were the tables to wipe, the cloths to spread out and anchor down, the new cushions to put in every chair, and she wanted a good sweeping before—

Wings fluttered in the air in front of her face. It was the robin. The bird had apparently taken her advice, the tabletop would not make the best place to raise her family, and now she was starting a nest in the spokes of one of the umbrellas.

"Not again." Amy skidded to a halt as the bird lighted on a chair back and glared right back at her.

"This is why I can't grow flowers or a vegetable garden. I can't chase anything off. Not the deer that walk right up to my home and eat my lilacs and carrot tops. Not even a bird who should know this is a bad place to build a nest." She looked at her watch. There was no way she had time to wage a battle of any kind. "Could I ask you—?"

"Sure." He moved past her, waving his free hand. "You have to find a better place, sorry."

The robin took one look at him and fluttered off, perhaps for good.

"Thank you. I'm running behind this morning." She had a nice smile, a sincere one, and he was glad he'd been able to help.

It felt good and solid in his chest. "Want me to set up here? I can do it."

"That would be great. I've got to run and pop the cinnamon rolls into the fridge. Oh, that reminds me. Do you attend church?"

It was a question simply spoken without judgment or expectation. But Heath felt a thud in the center of his chest, and it was as if everything inside him were falling. He gripped the chair for support as he tried to say without malice, "No. I don't attend."

"Okay. I would have offered you a ride, but if you'd rather stay, Jodi should be in any time. Oh—" Amy cocked her head, listening.

The tiny gold crosses at her earlobes winked in the sun. "Oh, here she is. I'll tell her you'll be here to help. I know she'll appreciate it."

In the next heartbeat, she was gone, going about her morning work as if it was just another Sunday morning, another day in her week. Leaving him alone to try to calm the rush of memories he could not stomach. Memories he did not want.

Up in the trees beyond the privacy wall and the tall lilac bushes, the robin chirped. The train rumbling by brought with it the last of the cars and its cabooses. He waited until the train's noise grew softer, until it was gone. He waited until the sounds of the morning, of the leaves and the birds and the clatter of dishes inside the diner crowded out the shadows.

Quietly, purposefully, he wiped down the tables, snapped the freshly laundered tablecloths into place and figured out the strange decorative clips that held the cloths down in the wind. He heard Amy's car start in the lot behind the restaurant and the tires rasp on the pavement as she drove away. He caught sight of her as she pulled onto the main road in front of the diner.

She waved, friendly but with that polished

manner of hers that kept her shield firmly in place. Cool and firm and polite. If he hadn't seen her with the wild bird, he never would have guessed she was such a sweetheart. So soft and good of spirit that wild birds did not fear her.

He knew, too, that he and Amy were more alike than different, and that was oddly surprising. A small-town waitress and a big-city doctor. Maybe that's why he felt as if he wanted to stay on. Because he saw a kindred spirit in Amy McKaslin. She, too, kept nearly everyone at a distance, kept safe. Did she, he wondered, recognize the same in him, too?

He wondered what pain she hid so carefully. She looked lovely, the kind of woman who'd probably had a golden life growing up in this cozy small town. Adored by her family, she probably had been a cheerleader and class valedictorian.

But that didn't make a person immune to tragedy. To pain. He knew from first-hand experience that no one had the perfect life, no matter how it seemed. There was no telling what scars were hidden deep inside a person.

Somewhere nearby church bells tolled, rich and resonant.

Feeling ties from the past, ones he could not face, he retreated inside. He shut the door behind him so he could no longer hear the bells.

While he treasured the silence, he felt no peace.

"…and then Mrs. Winkler said God made all the stars in the heavens." Westin paused to cough into his fist, straining against his car booster seat.

Amy glanced anxiously into the rearview mirror, but he looked fine. His color was good. His next breath came clear. Maybe the new medicine the specialist had prescribed was doing its job. *Please, Lord.* She wanted a normal childhood for her little boy. With all of her heart.

To her delight, Westin shook his head as he often did, and ran his fingers through his hair. The fine strands stood straight up from static electricity. He was beyond cute.

And he knew it, too. He gave a charming grin and kept on with his story. "I asked about the galaxies, too, and Mrs. Winkler said that the stars in the heavens means the galaxies, too, but she's wrong. I told her that galaxies are not stars. And that the galaxies are speeding away." He held up his hands as if he were holding a globe and pulled them apart. "She must not got any cable. Or she'd know that."

"Not everyone watches the science shows."

He looked crestfallen. "Me and George better pray for her so she can have cable." He grabbed his ragged Snoopy dog, which had been his favorite stuffed toy for most of his life.

"That's a good idea, baby."

"Yeah, I know." While squeezing George around his middle, Westin bowed his head. His lips moved in an earnest prayer.

She couldn't help keeping one eye on the mirror. Her little boy was her everything. She felt as if she shone from the inside out from simply watching him.

Since the morning was pleasant and sunny, she had her windows down. She had escaped a few minutes early from the overflowing church parking lot, and was already on her way along the tree-lined residential streets to work.

As she drove, Pastor Bill's sermon weighed on her; while she usually felt renewed and refreshed after Sunday service, she didn't today. Today she felt unsettled. She would have preferred a sermon that hadn't made her think of the man she'd hired. But the message and text had struck her hard, giving her a gnawing feeling that she could have handled things much better with Heath.

"Mom!" Westin squirmed, drawing her attention, all bridled energy. She marveled at how the seat belt managed to hold him still as he lunged against it and stretched his arm as far as possible so the stuffed dog popped up next to her head rest. "George wants strawberry waffles with the white stuff."

"Whipped cream. Not syrup? I thought George liked syrup."

"He changed his mind, but he wants lots of sausage."

"With syrup or ketchup?"

"Both!"

It was good to see her little one in good spirits—it was more than she could say for herself.

The Lord does not look at the things man looks at. Man looks at the outward appear-

ance, but the Lord looks at the heart. That was the text Pastor Bill had spoken on in his compassionate and compelling way. The verse from 1 Samuel wasn't something she'd read in a while—with Paige gone, she'd been too busy to make the last two weeks of her Bible study group, and with Westin's asthma peaking since Christmas, her attendance had been spotty. Maybe that's why today's passage had taken hold of her, as if her spirit was hungry.

Man looks at the outward appearance. Is that what she was guilty of? Making, if not judgments about Heath, then certainly assessments. He was down on his luck; it sure looked that way. He wore clean but far from new clothes. His truck was at least twenty years old.

But he'd left Jodi a good tip, and Rachel had said he'd worked hard when she'd called early in the morning to go over the week's work schedule she'd made.

"I don't know what Heath told you," Rachel had reported. "But he has a talent of understatement and a gift of modesty. I was prepared to work two jobs, training him and cooking, which, as you know, is demanding on our busiest night of the week. But he just took over. Ten minutes into the dinner rush, he was handling the grill like a pro."

"You're kidding." Amy had nearly dropped the phone as she rummaged through her dresser drawers looking for socks to match her tan trousers. Amy had assumed Heath was like so many others who passed through looking for work. Some were not to be trusted, but others, they had their reasons for wandering.

That's what she'd assumed about Heath. But she could only see his outward appearance. The Lord could look into everyone's heart, sure, but how could she? She knew from lessons learned that a man can show one face convincingly, but his motives and his agendas and his true nature can stay well hidden.

She zipped down the alley and into the back lot, recognizing the few cars parked there. Rachel hadn't beaten her here, but Cousin Kelly had, and the clatter and bang behind the screen door told her Jodi was busy already.

"Grab your backpack, please," she told her son as soon as she'd cut the engine and tucked the keys into her pants pocket.

"George is coming, too."

"Then hold him tight." Amy bent, jamming one knee on the back seat so she could help Westin. He squirmed and struggled and yanked on the buckle and bopped from the seat the instant he was free.

Amy backed up, waiting as he bounded from the car holding his stuffed dog around its middle and holding onto his backpack's strap with the other. She shut the door, remembered to grab her purse and followed him in.

Her boy bounded ahead of her, his backpack bouncing in rhythm to his gait and poor George, loose-limbed from years of being dragged around, jiggled like a rag doll. He yanked open the screen door with great zeal and the old hinges squealed in protest.

Westin skidded to a halt in midstride. "Hey! You're not supposed to be in here. Mom, he's a stranger."

Amy removed her sunglasses. Heath had his back to the grill, staring at Westin as if he'd never seen a child before. He probably hadn't realized she had a son. Maybe he hadn't noticed the pictures of Westin tacked in the little office, along with Paige's teenage boy's photos. "Heath, this is my son, Westin. Westin, what do you say?"

"I'm pleased to meet you, sir." Westin snapped to attention like a little soldier. He held out his dog. "And so is George. Did you know the star that's closest to the earth is called Alpha Centauri and it's four light years away?"

Instead of answering, Heath stared.

He was probably unaware of the exciting facts about space, so Amy ruffled Westin's head. "Go and find Kelly. She's waiting for you."

"Okay, Mom." He paused to cough quickly in his fist and kept on talking. "But light years aren't like real years. They're, like, way bigger. Light travels so fast it's like this. Zoom." He held his hand level and, imitating a rocket, his hand shot upward. "That's fast."

"Uh, yeah." Heath looked bewildered.

She couldn't blame him. He'd probably spent little or no time around children. "Go. Quick. I've got to get to work."

"Okay, but I got this book in here," he tapped on his backpack, "and it's about our space and stuff. Did you know—"

"Go," Amy interrupted. "You'd better hurry. I bet George is hungry."

"Oh, yeah! George always wants sausages." Westin took off for the double doors, giving them a mighty shove so they smacked against the wall and swung back and forth hard.

She caught glimpses of him dashing over to Kelly at a booth, where her college books lay open before her. Her face lit up with greeting and she gave George and Westin kisses on their cheeks. With her son being cared for, now she could turn her thoughts to work.

But Heath had returned to the grill, stirring scrambled eggs with the spatula as if it took every bit of his concentration. His back was an insurmountable barrier between them.

Maybe he didn't like children. Or maybe the issue was with her. Lord help her, she could not forget what he'd said to her so cruelly. *Whatever it is you're thinking you can get from me, forget it.* He was a good-looking man. Perhaps he was used to women thinking they'd be the ones to land him. To put a ring on his finger and chain him down in one place.

She didn't know. Before her old bitterness

could surge up, she tasted it sour in the back of her throat. She didn't want to be bitter, but it wasn't easy. She'd tried so long and hard to forgive herself for her shameful mistakes, and Lord knew she did her best to forgive the man who'd hurt her so thoroughly. But remnants remained, flaring up like those geyser firestorms in the sun.

The Lord looks at the heart. Pastor Bill's understanding voice filled her head as she washed her hands in the sink. She couldn't see into anyone's heart, not really, but there were probably clues. She watched out of the corner of her eye as she tore off a length of paper towel to dry with. Heath worked sure and efficiently, making omelets now, squinting to read Jodi's scrawl on a ticket before fetching a new package of sausage links from the fridge.

"Looks like you have everything under control." She had to approach him because her apron was hanging on a hook next to the refrigerator. "Let me know when you need a hand. It always takes two at the grill on brunches."

"Okay." He lifted one wide shoulder in a

shrug, not exactly careless, but the message was clear: stay back.

She could respect that. In fact, she preferred it. A polite and efficient working relationship worked for her. She reached around to tie a bow at the small of her back as he passed by her. The faint aroma of soap and spicy aftershave made something stir inside her. A yearning for the life with a husband she'd always dreamt of. The comforting hugs, the sizzling kisses, the shared closeness.

It was odd she'd feel any longing for that old, spent dream. She had too many years under her belt to believe romantic love existed. Maybe that's what women wanted to believe. Maybe it's what they needed to believe.

Every once in awhile, it probably did happen. She'd see it now and then, the genuine tie of deep affection that bound husbands and wives together. It was like the glow of dust in the night sky Westin had shown her, the spiral arm of their Milky Way. A soft luminous miracle. True love ought to shine like that.

But miracles were rare. She'd learned for

sure that the fall was not worth the risk. She'd already had one miracle in her life, she thought, as she pushed through the doors and checked on the number of empty tables. As Rachel rushed in the front door to help seat families, Amy spotted Westin, hunched over a book on the table, showing Kelly something very important on the page.

She had her one miracle in life. It was enough.

On her way to check on the status of the buffet, she stopped to say hello to her cousins—Kendra was nice enough to have already copied off the video of Westin's game. Her uncle Pete and aunt Alice always had a kind word to say to her. There were friends from school with families of their own now, with their greetings. She received many compliments on the food.

She fetched fresh fruit trays from the fridge, warmed cinnamon rolls to set out, helped with the coffee refills while Rachel, late and breathless, took over hostess duties. She checked on Westin and George—their order of strawberry waffles and sausages had been a big hit.

The diner hummed with the scrape of flatware and the ring of stoneware and the cheerful rise and fall of conversations. Kids clamored around the dessert table, excited by the choices while their parents talked and leisurely went for seconds from the buffet. Neighbors and friends would stop to talk in the aisles, and through the order-up window Amy could see Heath, cap on, his attention focused on his work. She never saw him look up at the crowd, only to read order tickets or Rachel's scrawl on what was running low at the buffet.

"Oh, the crepes were divine." Kelly pulled her aside. "I see you have a new cook. He's great."

"That's what everybody's been saying." She felt arms wrap around her waist and hold on.

It was her son with his big grin and sparkling eyes who gave her a tight squeeze and then hopped away. "George and I have to go, Mom!"

"You two be good for Kelly." The sight of her little boy walking out of her sight tugged at her, as it always did. Already she missed him.

Pastor Bill and his wife were the last of the

after-church crowd to arrive, as usual, looking composed and happy and friendly. It was impossible not to want to give them a hug, which Amy did, and offered them their choice of available tables. They wanted outside beneath the umbrellas, for the afternoon was a beautiful one.

This is why she was so grateful to live in this small rural town in the middle of farming country. It was far from the bustle of larger, urban centers that as a teenage girl she'd thought were exciting. But she'd been wrong.

Roots. Family. Community. There was no place like home. No place.

And what about Heath? The talented cook fate—or, more correctly, God—had sent their way. He worked so well, he needed no help on the busiest of times and he kept to himself, alone, lost in shadows.

Jodi was wrong. There was more than a great sorrow about him, wrapping him up like a blanket. It was so sharp and agonizing, Amy could feel it radiating off him like heat from an August sidewalk.

Through the order-up window and across the length of the diner, their gazes met.

Locked. A jolt of blackness shocked her so deep in her heart it forced the air from her lungs.

Unable to blink and unable to look away, she gasped for breath. Shocked, she realized it was his heart she saw before he turned his back, breaking the connection.

He did not look her way again.

Chapter Seven

Heath couldn't get the image out of his mind. The image of Amy McKaslin with her son. He hadn't guessed that she was a mom. Nope, he couldn't reconcile it. Maybe because he didn't want to.

All through the afternoon and into the evening he worked. The diner closed at eight, early on Sunday nights. There had been no place open on the six-block length of the main street, except the dark-tinted neon lights in the far alley at the edge of town   the tavern.

He knew how it would be inside that dim, small building. The air would be soured with smoke where men sucked down alcohol to hide from their troubles. There'd be darts and a pool table—nothing worth going in for. He'd seen it all before and he wasn't interested.

He'd learned the hard way. There wasn't anything strong enough to obliterate his problems or anesthetize his pain, so he climbed the stairs to his apartment and sat in the tepid current of the window air conditioner and watched a movie of the week on the TV. He played with the rabbit ears until he had a pretty good picture and not much static.

That night he tossed and turned as dark images haunted him. He woke as wet as if he'd been drowning in the Atlantic waters, sweat sluicing down his face and stinging in his eyes.

The television mumbled in the background—he must have fallen asleep on the couch. The place was hot and the walls seemed to be closing in on him. He did the only thing he could and launched straight to the door, yanked it open and dropped to the steps. Gulped in the cool night air.

A train gave a long low note of warning as it rumbled through town. The rhythmic hum of engines and the grinding on the steel tracks hid the calm night. It was like the noise of a city, traffic and a background hum that never silenced.

For an instant Heath's mind hooked him back into the past: the whine of trucks downshifting on the interstate had accompanied him as he'd bounded out of the emergency-room doors, rain pouring down his face, slick beneath his shoes, glossing the blacktop of the Portland hospital's emergency zone. Images assaulted him: ambulances' strobes, the hustle of the team, the bright crimson splash of blood on the sheet-covered gurney—

Thunder exploded like a gunshot, startling him out of the past. He let the cold and wind wash over him. Breathed in the metallic scent of thunder and waited for the lightning to flare.

There it was, a jagged finger thrust from the sky to the distant fields. One, two, three, four…

I gotta get out of here Thunder crashed like metal through the iridescent clouds. Heath swiped the wetness from his face, not sure if it was only rain. How had he made such a big mistake? He never would have taken the job if he'd known about the boy.

That's what he got for acting on impulse. For thinking he could stay awhile. What was it about those big blue eyes of Amy's that made him feel as if he'd be all right?

He was alone. He was always going to be alone. There would never be anyone to understand, anyone to turn to and no chance to change the past and make things right. He'd give his life, his soul, everything and anything if only he could go back in time to that crucial moment on another night of rain and thunder. Change one little second. One tiny decision. If only...

There were no "if only"s. The past was done with. He'd been over it a hundred billion times. Looking back wouldn't bring him closer to what he deserved.

Leave. That's what he'd do. He hated to run out on Amy, when she'd been worried he was the type of man who would do just that. He let the wind and rain blow him through the front door and it took less than two minutes to jam the few possessions he'd removed from the worn duffel bag back into it. With a final zip, he was done. He settled the strap on his shoulder and turned off the window unit and the TV, feeling lower than low.

It was a cheap shot, taking off without so much as a note.

What would he say to the McKaslins? Leave them a note that he'd made a mistake and to keep his paycheck. Brunch and the Sunday supper crowd had brought in enough tips to give him adequate traveling cash.

As the cold rain and violent night enveloped him, he dug his truck keys from his pocket. Rain streaked down his face and got into his eyes. With his free hand he wiped at his face and almost missed the sound of glass breaking.

At first he thought it came from the alley, maybe from the direction of the old woman's house, but he heard it again. He swore the crashing sound of shattering glass came right behind him. But that didn't make any sense. Who'd be out in this storm? Lightning shot like a flare from west to east and reflected in a bright flash on a vehicle's windshield.

Then darkness reclaimed the night. Rain pelted with wild abandon from a hateful sky beating Heath back as he tossed his duffel to the ground at the bottom of the stairs and ran around the front. Wet branches hung low with the weight of the rain and sodden leaves slapped his face and head. He didn't stop. Thunder drowned out the sound of a loud cowboylike holler somewhere near the front door.

Heath knew who those men were before he skidded around the corner in a patch of loose gravel, so he wasn't a bit surprised when he saw the two lowlifes he'd chased off before. They stood side by side without a coat or heavy shirt against the mean storm, laughing with their hands full of big rocks.

"This here is for the deputy comin' by my place." The taller one pitched a heavy rock through the window.

Heath cringed at the tinkling sound of shattering glass. Rain spilled through the jagged, gaping hole in the window. Fury hurling him forward, he tore into the open like a wild man. Heath's vision turned red as he tackled both men and rolled them out on the road.

"Hey, man!" one of the troublemakers held up his hands, surrendering. Blood stained his hair where he'd hit the curb.

"This ain't your business!" The other twisted onto his feet, shook off the rain and raised both fists. "You want to fight, we'll fight—"

The strong scent of cheap whisky and cheaper vodka tainted the wind. All Heath could think was that it was guys like this. They were responsible. Drinking and careless, their judgement impaired. Savage wrath choked him. How did these people do it? How could it be entertaining to hurt someone? How could there be any satisfaction in destroying someone's life? He wanted vengeance. He wanted justice. He wanted his life back.

And men like these. They were responsible—

Headlights sheened on the black river of road and the splashing sound of tires hydroplaning on a skid snapped him back to himself. He felt tall and terrible and broken. Endlessly broken.

Vaguely he was aware of the cruiser door opening, black rain falling like bullets, the thugs shouting and taking off. Their footsteps pounded across the road where water ran like a river and another cruiser squealed to a stop nearby, headlights blaring as another officer joined the hunt. Heath was only a half step behind, his military training kicking in, but in the few seconds it took to cross the road, he saw the two drunks on the ground, facedown in the mud on the other side of the railroad tracks.

"Not the brightest guys," Frank explained later, after the two had been cuffed and hauled away in the sheriff's car. "Down at the tavern they talked about what they were gonna do here. One of the waitresses heard the whole thing and called me the minute those two were out the door. Good thing, too. Look at this."

Frank shook his head in disgust at the damage. "It's not too late yet. I'll give John a call and see if he'll open up the hardware store."

Heath's guts twisted looking at the damage. Two sections had been broken out of the large front windows, glass reflecting darkly with the rain and the night. There was only one thing to do. "I'm fairly good with a hammer. I figure I can get this boarded up before—"

Headlights pierced the black storm, coming as if out of nowhere. Heath knew it was Amy even before the dome light flashed on to reveal her face pinched and pale. She'd drawn her hair back in a quick ponytail and a shank of hair lay twisted and at an angle over her cowlick. The storm deluged her in the ten seconds it took for her to race through the light beams to the sidewalk.

"Careful." He held out his arm to stop her. "Glass."

"Oh, yeah." She hadn't looked down. Dazed, she froze, staring at the wreckage with rainwater sluicing down her face, wetting her hair so that even the shank trying to stand up became slicked to her head. Her coat clung to her willowy frame and she looked younger, much too young to be a mother of a grade-school boy. She looked so vulnerable it made Heath's rage flare again.

"They'll pay for this," he ground out, his hands finding the curves of her shoulders. "Every penny. I'll make sure of it."

"It's not just the glass. Oh, look, it's just so much damage."

Her reaction came so quietly, without hysteria or upset or anger. Beneath his hands, the rounded curve of her shoulders quivered— with fear or repressed anger or just from the cold he couldn't tell. She was fragile, feminine and small—and as he towered behind her to block her from the brunt of the icy rain, his chest jolted from the inside out. It was as if the locked door had been wrenched open a scant inch and feeling poured through him.

"Paige is going to split a seam when she sees this. She just got back tonight—" She sounded lost, as if she didn't have the first clue where to start. "What about breakfast? We won't be able to open."

"We'll get it boarded up. Frank—" Heath glanced around, but the deputy was nowhere to be seen. His car idled along the curb where he'd left it. Maybe he was making the phone call to the hardware-store owner. "I'm here anyway. I might as well take care of it."

"No, this isn't your problem. That's good of you, but, oh, I don't think we're insured for something like this. We only have basic liability."

Solid. He hadn't felt like this since the old days. Steady and calm and ready to handle what came. He saw the ghost of the man he used to know inside him as lightning flashed. In the brief illumination, he saw his reflection in the shattered window. Cracked and distorted, black in places, that was him. There was no way to repair damage like that.

It wasn't like a window a worker could remove from its frame and fit in a new one as good as new.

No, the human spirit wasn't like that.

As swift as the lightning came, it vanished, the brilliant white light receding into the darkness. But the hole—the void inside him—remained. Which did he choose? The void or the light? The road rolled out behind him, gleaming darkly with streaming water, gurgling like a current toward the edge of town and beyond.

I want that path. He craved oblivion like an addiction. Desperately he'd take anything to stop the feelings flowing through him like the floodwater, fast and ruthless. His duffel bag was within reach, sitting in a puddle, and it would be nothing at all to grab it up and go. No, he'd fix her windows first, then go. He'd be safe, he'd never have to remember—

She sniffed, wiped at her eyes with the tip of her finger and let out a shaky breath. He didn't know why, but he could feel the wave of her shock rolling through him like an ocean tide. Rolling higher until he was full of it. He did not want to be the one to comfort her. He didn't want to be the man she turned to, because her need and her touch would make him real again, would make him alive again. All he wanted was the night and the darkness.

He deserved nothing more.

"There's no sense in you standing in the rain." He took one long look at his drenched duffel bag, knowing this would take him where he didn't want to go. But he couldn't walk away. "C'mon, let's get you inside."

She fumbled in her pocket. "Oh, they're in my car. The keys."

Crestfallen. That's how she looked, staring in disbelief. "Nobody's hurt. That's the important thing. It's just glass. It can be fixed. I don't know why I'm so shook up."

"You and your sisters don't deserve this, that's why." He hated leaving her, but it gave him time to let the cold settle across his face. Breathing deep, he let the night batter him and knock its way inside until he felt icy calm.

He killed the engine and took the keys, flicked off the headlights and shut the door. The street was flooded, and his splashing steps gave him something to think about other than the woman standing alone and the road whispering to take him away.

"What are you?" She studied him with fathomless eyes, shadowed and unreadable as he unlocked the front door, the bottom half shattered.

"What am I? Most people ask who." He gave the rock on the carpet a shove with his foot and swept the big shards of glass out of a path with the side of his boot. With care, so he wouldn't get cut. The big chunks scraped out of the way,

"Careful," he told her as she inched by him, her shoulder warm and wet against his chest.

"Oh, look at this. What is wrong with people?" The first flush of a healthy fury spread across her cheeks. "I can't thank you enough for being here. You probably stopped this from being a whole lot worse."

"I don't know about that." Guilt kept him from saying the truth. The rain hammering the roof echoed and amplified the sound in the empty restaurant. "Right place at the right time, I guess."

"You have a knack f-for it," she said as her teeth chattered.

He cradled her small hands between his. "You're ice. Sit. I'll get you something hot."

"Oh, n-no, you don't have to wait on me. I can—"

"You didn't even wear a warm jacket." He released her hands and peeled off the thin coat, more like a windbreaker than anything. No wonder she was borderline hypothermic. "Sit."

"But I—"

"Don't argue." The words came out harsher than he'd intended. Her eyes rounded and she dropped into the nearest booth.

He shouldn't be taking his feelings out on her. This wasn't her fault. He still wanted to leave. Maybe it was better if he did. He could talk to her some, tell her enough so she'd understand. Yeah, it sounded like a plan, but it didn't set right in his stomach as he flipped on the light and went in search of the right ingredients.

"If a wild-eyed woman comes bursting through the door, don't call Frank. It's my sister Paige. She's used to being in charge. I'm warning you before she shows up so you're prepared."

The pot clanked on the burner. "Why do I need to be prepared?"

"Because you look at me, Rachel and Jodi funny."

"What do you mean by funny?"

"Like you're wondering how fast you can make it to the door."

"You mean, in case of a fire?"

Amy swiped the wet bangs plastered to her face. He was going to joke, was he? She couldn't believe it. "Are you denying it?"

"Yep." Clangs came from deep inside the shadowed kitchen. He'd turned on only the small light over the sink, and the rip of the refrigerator door opening had her wondering what he was fixing.

"Hot tea is fine. Maybe I should—"

"Stay." His command was firm.

If she wasn't still so shaky, she'd give him a piece of her mind. Amy Marie McKaslin did not take orders from any man.

Not ever again.

The diner phone rang. Her sisters knew she was here. She'd promised to call right away and report in, but she had yet to do it. She knew Paige would be rushing here, driving as fast as the storm would allow. So that left Rachel at home with Westin wondering what had happened. Talking to her sister sure sounded like a good idea. She'd feel a lot better just to hear Rachel's voice.

But Heath beat her to the phone, turning his strong back toward her and cradling the receiver against his ear. His deep baritone rumbled low and the storm blowing inside made it impossible to hear his words.

What she needed to do was to get up and start cleaning up. The damage was ugly, but it could be made right so they could open tomorrow. That wasn't what had hit her so hard.

It was the shock of seeing the destruction. It was as if the past had come back around. Seeing the black reflective shards on the carpet made her remember, when she didn't want to ever think about that time in her life again.

Heath ambled toward her, as shadowed as the night surrounding him, and stood just shy of the fall of light through the door. He made a fine picture standing there like something out of a movie. Wet dark hair was plastered to his scalp, his face was damp, his jacket clung to his linebacker's shoulders and his worn black jeans were snug against his long lean legs.

He swiped his fingers through his hair. "That was the deputy. The store owner told him where the spare key was hidden and said to help ourselves."

"That would be John through and through. He's one of the good guys."

"The way you say that makes it sound like we're far and few."

"I didn't know you were one of the good guys." Her throat ached and she looked away. She'd meant to tease, but it had backfired on her. She'd long ago given up trying to figure out which were the genuine men and which were the ones in sheep's clothing. She hardly knew Heath…did she even know his last name? Rachel had given him paperwork to fill out, not that Amy had had time to look.

He said nothing more. His waterlogged boots squished as he left. Amy rubbed her face, but that didn't help the pain building behind her forehead or the fact she had a long night ahead of her. What she ought to do is start cleaning up the glass. Get it out of the way so she could board up the windows.

It felt better to have a plan and it gave her something else to think about besides the man in the kitchen rescuing a cup from the microwave. She could see him at work at the counter—stirring something into the steaming cup, reaching up to search through the cupboard, standing at attention like a soldier as he contemplated his choices.

"I love any kind of tea," she told him, pushing off the booth's bench seat and finding out her legs were steady again. She hadn't taken two steps when Heath shouldered through the doors with one of the huge latte mugs in hand.

"Where do you think you're going? Sit down and drink this. No, it's not tea."

He meant business, she could see that. His gaze pinned hers with a no-nonsense look. His jaw drew tight. He looked about as easy to push over as a heavyweight boxing champion. "It's hot chocolate?"

"With everything on it but a cherry, because I couldn't find any in the pantry."

"I can't believe you did this." She hardly looked at the rich cocoa heaped with whipped cream and dribbled with chocolate. "I thought you were nuking some tea water."

"No, this is better." He fumbled, self-conscious, as he slid the brimming cup before her.

"I'll say. Thank you."

"It's what my mom always made me when I was down and out." And my wife, he didn't add. There was a lot he didn't add. "I told Frank I'd come over and help him. We'll get a couple of pieces of plywood in place, and that'll keep out the rain and any skunks or creatures looking to get out of the rain."

"I'm perfectly capable of helping, too. This is my family's diner. I ought to—"

"No. The hot chocolate will warm you up. You've got a heavy load to carry, being a single mom. And I—" His chest hitched and he didn't want to care. He didn't. So he said nothing more and backed away toward the door, feeling the night and the endless road calling to him.

A tall, brown-haired woman with Amy's big blue eyes and nearly the same delicate structure to her face climbed out of the storm, crunching across glass on heavy, tooled riding boots. "What is wrong with people? I leave for a week and this place falls apart. Who are you?"

"The cook." He slipped past her, figuring this had to be the oldest sister everyone had talked about.

Paige McKaslin gave him one measuring glance, seemed to find him below par and dismissed him with an efficient shake of her head. "Amy? What's going on here? I know our insurance isn't going to cover this."

Heath left the sisters alone and took refuge in the endless night. The rain was calming, but the storm had tossed broken tree branches into the road. The big round headlight of the oncoming train seemed to hover eerily in the dark gleaming night.

He rescued his duffel; everything inside had to be sopping wet. He hefted the strap and water gushed out from the bottom of the bag. He tossed it under the eaves at the apartment door and a motion caught his attention in the shadowed window.

Amy moved away, her arms wrapped around her middle.

He understood without knowing why that she'd seen the bag. She knew that he'd packed and would leave her high and dry without a cook, just as she'd feared he would. Her disappointment rolled like fog misting up from a river. It shamed him, but there were worse things.

She didn't wake at night, locked in a nightmare without end and hearing the cries of her child dying, the way he did.

He prayed to God she never would.

Chapter Eight

Amy sat in her car, shivering in the chilly dampness. Paige's black SUV blended with the dark world, the taillights floating pinpoints of light as smokelike fog rose from the sodden earth like thousands of souls to heaven.

Amy had felt much better after Heath's cup of cocoa. The rich velvety brew had melted the shock from her system and warmed her up enough for her synapses to start firing again. She'd helped Heath and Frank hold and nail the sheets of plywood, while Paige swept up the glass, and, with a wet vac, dried up most of the rain damage.

Except for the two booths nearest the door, every table was fine. They'd be open for breakfast bright and early at 6:00 a.m. as usual, which, according to her battered sports watch, was two hours and five minutes away. She could snatch a little sleep—it wouldn't be much, but some was better than none. It sounded like a good idea, but the dark windows above the diner kept drawing her attention.

She remembered how hard Heath had worked alongside Frank, competently driving nails with a hammer as if he'd been a carpenter somewhere along the line. She could picture it, him in a hard hat, a T-shirt and jeans, thick heavy boots and a carpenter's belt at his hips. His face, neck and arms were sun-browned, as if he'd worked outside in his last job.

So, what was he doing working as a cook? He'd make so much more as a union trades-man. And why was his bag packed and dropped, as if he'd been on his way out for good without so much as a goodbye, just as she'd pegged him for.

Yeah, she could pick 'em. The only type of man she seemed to attract was the kind that left. Commitment-shy, free-and-easy, or simply wanting an entanglement-free life.

That's why she'd given up hoping she'd ever find a good man to marry. She had a son, she had a mortgage payment and she had responsibilities to her sisters that went beyond part ownership of the restaurant.

Responsibility was a concept few men grasped—maybe it was just the effect of testosterone on the brain. Whatever it was, she'd found out it was easier and safer to keep every single one of them at a reasonable distance. Tonight had been illuminating for very good reasons—every time she began to weaken God had a way of reminding her.

Deeply grateful, she shivered in the cool blow of the defroster, waiting for the engine to warm up. If she closed her eyes, she could still see it. The smashed window crisscrossed with fractures like a giant spider's web. The dresser's mounted mirror in the little bedroom she'd rented in an older neighborhood in Seattle's university district. The tiny window in the front door. The windshield of her car. Glass shards cutting her bare feet as she hurried to sweep them up. From her favorite little juice glasses with the daisies on them. From a beer bottle thrown against the kitchen wall.

It was important to remember. Never to

forget. She already had what she needed. Her son. Her family. There was no need to look for more. She had enough. More than she thought she deserved, and that made her grateful.

As for Heath—the image remained of his shadow moving across the darker background of the storm, rescuing his duffel bag from the wet ground and taking it back upstairs. Had he changed his mind about leaving? Or was he merely getting his pack out of the rain?

It was probably the latter. Men left. It's what they did. He'd taken one look at her son and leaped to the wrong conclusion, thinking that she was on the hunt for a husband. Isn't that what a working single mom wanted? A man to foot the bills so she wouldn't have to?

If she had a nickel for every time someone advised her to start dating so she didn't have to work so hard, she'd be able to buy her own four-star restaurant on the Seattle waterfront, like she'd always dreamed of.

The last thing she wanted or needed was another man to tell her what was wrong with her, to take over her life and destroy it and run off with every last cent she owned. Whether Heath was that sort of man or not, it didn't make one bit of difference. She wasn't interested.

But maybe he didn't understand that. The way he'd avoided looking at her after he returned from the hardware store with Frank had said it all. The more she thought about it, the angrier she got. She'd do better to take a deep breath, chill out and forget it. Let him leave. She'd get up in… She glanced at the clock, okay, less than two hours' time and man the grill. It was no big deal.

Then why was she so angry?

Because it was easier to feel anger than to face the truth, to pull up the memory of Heath standing at the grill after Westin had talked to him. She'd somehow seen inside him at that moment, to where his heart was as dark as the center of a black hole, a place that allowed no light, nothing but an endlessly collapsing void. What could cause that kind of pain?

She saw the flicker of a movement at the window. It had to be him. She imagined him gazing, not at her but in the opposite direction. Looking east where the road led. Did he regret staying long enough to help her and her sisters out—again?

A lot of men wouldn't have bothered to get involved at all. But he had. He'd chosen to stay when he could have walked away. Was he up there alone in the utter darkness without the benefit of a single light on, wishing he'd made another choice? Making plans to leave with the dawn?

She didn't know why, but if he left that way, she would have regrets. There would always be the feeling that she'd left something undone.

For all his good deeds to her, she'd done nothing in return. Everything within her felt at war. She didn't want to get close to any man—and yet there was something in Heath that tugged at her as if a line ran from his soul to hers. Why else could she feel his pain? See the infinite void within his heart?

She ought to go home, and yet she knew if she did Heath would be gone by morning and she would never know—what, she wasn't sure. She knew she already cared about Heath too much. More than was safe. More than was sensible for a woman with her luck. And yet, she would never rest easy if he were gone come sunrise. *Show me what to do, Lord. Please, I need your guidance.*

Then again, maybe He'd given her enough already. She was exhausted and thinking in circles. She had a son to get home to.

"Car trouble?"

Amy recognized Heath's voice even as adrenaline jetted into her bloodstream and her hand was curling around the strap of her purse to use it as a weapon. He'd scared ten years off her life.

She shoved open the door. "Would you stop doing that?"

"Want to hit the hood lock for me, and I'll take a look." He flicked on a flashlight, the small beam reflected with eye-stinging brightness in the thick fog. "What's the problem?"

"In order for the car to go, the driver has to put it into gear."

"You mean you've been sitting here on purpose? It's almost four in the morning and it's starting to freeze. The roads are already dangerous enough."

"I never thanked you for the hot chocolate."

"That can't be why you're sitting out here

alone in the dark. Even in a town like this, it can't be entirely safe." The mist turned into translucent flakes as the water froze in midair, shrouding him with a strange dark light. It made Amy remember how he'd seemed in the kitchen after Westin had left.

"Maybe I'd better drive you," he offered.

"I'm not afraid of a little ice on the road. Goodness, I learned to drive in the winter."

That polite shield again. Heath took in Amy's picture-perfect smile—not too wide, not too bright but just enough. There was nothing appreciably different about her, she was still wearing her thin jacket, and at least it had dried hanging above the heat duct in the restaurant. Her hair was still yanked unevenly back in a quick ponytail that was beginning to sag. Her flannel pajamas were very eye-catching.

"Isn't that Saturn?"

"As you may have noticed, my little boy is into astronomy. He got me these for Christmas this year. Wasn't that thoughtful? They are the softest jammies I've ever had."

They sure looked soft, quality combed flannel bottoms fell to the tops of her sneakers, and he was shocked that he noticed the way her slim ankle showed, just a bit. She was wearing knitted cable socks that would have made anyone else's ankles look less than slender and shapely.

Not that he ought to be noticing Amy's ankles—or any woman's.

He rubbed his left hand, where the ring hadn't been ever since he'd tossed it off the bridge after leaving the hospital. When he'd almost gone in the water with the ring.

Lord knew he hadn't had the courage then. He'd been naive enough still to believe that there would be hope somewhere, someday. Hope for what, he couldn't have said. Maybe it seemed impossible that something so sudden and horrific could be real.

He'd been in too much shock to realize that traumatic things happened all the time. Bad things happening to other people is what had made him, if not well off, then doing better than most. A new car, a nice house, a boat for Sunday afternoons on the lake.

But time had shown him one thing. His losses were real, death was final and his grief and guilt were never going to end. Every day since, he'd regretted not jumping off the bridge when he'd had the chance.

Although he wasn't much of a churchgoer, not any more, he was still a believer. And his faith taught that it was against God's law for a man to take his own life…in the end, as much as he'd wanted it, Heath had not been able to choose his own death.

Not that he had chosen to live either. He'd stopped being alive in every way that mattered long ago. What he wanted was oblivion—to keep from remembering, from feeling, to hide from the guilt that rose up like a tsunami. How could he have oblivion if everywhere he went, children made him remember? It wasn't Amy's fault that she was lucky enough to be a mom, that her little boy was alive and well, that he'd picked out pajamas for his mom with a planet design and he was as cute a little boy as Heath had ever seen.

And looking at Amy's son led Heath down the only obvious path. If Christian had lived, what would he have been interested in? Planes? Or trucks? Football or baseball? Would he color with those big chunky crayons made for little kids or would he prefer to finger paint? Would his big brown eyes have sparkled with joy over pancakes and sausages? Would he carry around a stuffed toy everywhere he went?

The tsunami overtook him, obliterating him. Heath took the hit and tried not to let it show. He didn't trust his voice, so he didn't say anything. It was better just to let it pass. It always did…eventually.

"Look at you." There was sympathy in her dulcet voice and her grip settled around his wrist, but it felt distant as if she were touching him through yards of Jell-O.

"What are you doing up at this hour to notice that I'm freezing to death in my car?"

He didn't answer. The air he breathed in scorched the linings of his nose and sinuses and stung deep in his chest. Maybe he could be like the fog, freeze up and just let the pain slide right off his soul.

"You did so much for us tonight." She left the engine idling as she stood and, shivering, searched him as if trying to figure out what was going on inside his skull.

It was private, not her business. He watched the ice particles in the air fall like the tiniest specks of snow and cling to her hair and eyelashes and melt against the softest creamiest skin he'd ever seen on a woman. Her soul shone in her eyes, and as she studied him, he felt as if the deepest part of him had been revealed. Without words. Without communication of any kind.

Sadness shadowed her eyes. "Let me take you upstairs."

"What about your boy?"

"He's asleep in his bed, and he'll be fine for a few hours more. After Rachel came over to look through the books with Paige, we got to talking. Suddenly it was midnight and so she made up a bed on the air mattress. She does it all the time, which worked out fine tonight, since the tavern called to let me know they'd called the cops and it was providential she was there to stay with Westin."

"That's pretty amazing. Frank told me he'd been called by someone hearing threats." Heath felt as cold as the outside air. "Not a lot of folks would get involved like that."

"We're a small community. I send the tavern a lot of business, you know, tourists looking for cocktails or a cold beer after a hot day in the car. We don't have a liquor license, so I send customers over. They do the same. It works out. I guess it's a small-town thing. Now, will you go upstairs before we both freeze? Or will I have to carry you up?"

"You've got to be kidding. I bet you've got a steel core, Amy McKaslin, but there's no way you can carry me up the stairs. I'll drive you home."

"I don't need a chauffeur."

"Humor me. I won't get a wink of sleep unless I know you're home safe."

"I'll call—wait, you don't have a phone." Amy shook her head, scattering the tiny wisps of golden silk that had escaped her disheveled ponytail. She looked like a waif in her too big coat and her flannel pants. "I'll be all right."

"You never know that for sure. You can take all the precautions you want, but sometimes it doesn't matter. So, do me this favor, okay?"

"Driving me home isn't a favor."

She didn't understand. He didn't need any "should-have"'s that resulted in more tragedy. He prodded her around the hood of the frosty sedan. The blacktop and then the concrete sidewalk beneath his feet were slick. "Is this my imagination, or is it snowing?"

"It's snowing."

"It's May."

"Welcome to Montana."

At least Amy's nearness gave him something else to think about. She smelled faintly of hot chocolate and shampoo and of the spring snow caught in her hair. A small blanket of faint freckles lay across her nose and cheeks, but that wasn't what made her cute. What drew him and held him was the quiet lock of her gaze on his. Although she said nothing, he sensed it. She'd seen the duffel bag, of course. She knew what he intended to do. She ought to be angry, but she wasn't.

"You have to wrench on it or it won't open." Her hand bumped his as she grabbed onto the door handle. "Just yank—there it goes. It sticks."

"I see."

Her car was pretty old. They'd stopped making this model, oh, about ten years ago, he figured, not that he was a car expert. But she kept it clean and in good repair. As he held the door while she settled into the bucket seat, he noticed it was clean and repaired with duct tape, which wasn't so noticeable on the gray upholstery.

She wasn't raking in the bucks at the family diner. He didn't need to see her car to know that. The restaurant did a healthy business, but this was a small town. It sounded as if it supported three sisters and their families, and it couldn't be easy.

He thought of the life he'd left. The suburban acreage in Lake Oswego, a nice tree-filled suburb of Portland. He'd even had a stretch of lakefront beach. It was a view his wife had loved. It was why he'd bought her the house. Thinking of home made his knees go watery as he crunched through the ice and snow to the driver's side. The house was gone. Everything was gone. Even if he wanted to, there was no going back.

She waited until they were safely across the railroad tracks and a few blocks from her trailer park. "Are you going to tell me why you're so eager to go?"

"You aim straight, don't you?"

"I don't see any point in pretending I didn't see the bag. You were going to slip out, weren't you, when you came across those horrible men."

"That's pretty much what happened." He kept his gaze on the road. It was tricky, he had to go slow because the fog absorbed the light and reflected it back, so the town streets were nearly invisible. Plus, he wasn't familiar with this stretch of highway.

He didn't offer more of an explanation. He figured she deserved to rant and rave or silently fume…or just accept it—whatever she needed to do. He was wrong. There was no denying it.

Amy McKaslin had a real life. What would she know about his? She had sisters and a business and a son, maybe more kids. He didn't know. She didn't wear a wedding ring, so he figured she was divorced. His guess was that she struggled to make ends meet, like any family.

He really didn't want to know anything else about her. He was already part of the fog, rolling with the rising wind. Already anticipating the dawn and the snowy drive through the state. Where he landed next was anyone's guess.

He'd leave it up to fate, or God, if He was still noticing.

"You'll need to turn right up here." Amy broke the silence and leaned forward against the restraint of the shoulder harness to help look along the road's shoulder. "There's the sign. Right here."

He caught a flash of a small sign, the kind apartments and house developments use. Oak Place, it said in snow-mantled letters on a spotty green background. He followed the narrower lane along a windrow of shrubs and turned, as Amy indicated, by a line of small mailboxes mounted on a two-by-four.

He saw the first trailer house. It was neat and maintained, but a good thirty years old. Then a second, newer one. And more, all quaintly lined up along the road, windows dark except for the occasional floodlight blinking on as the car drove by.

"Mine's the one with the rose arbor. Just pull in under the awning."

He did, noticing the single-wide was modest, and its front yard was white with snow. Another vehicle, which he remembered was Rachel's, had nosed in beneath a makeshift carport, and the whole passenger's side was covered with ice and snow.

"Home sweet home." Amy reached for her purse from the floor behind his seat. "Did you want to come in? I'll make you hot chocolate this time."

"No, I just wanted to see you were safe."

"So you could leave?"

"Something like that."

Amy wished she could be angry with him, but it wasn't that easy. How could she be angry with someone that wonderful? He spoke so well and knew how to make hollandaise sauce without checking a recipe and stood tall when danger called. Not the usual wanderer looking for a job. And that left the question, why? She instinctively knew it was a question that would only make him turn away.

Some things were better left in the past where they belonged. She thought of the foolish girl she used to be. Everyone deserved at least one free pass, one "do over." Maybe that's the way it was for Heath.

"If you want to come in for a second, I'll write you a paycheck."

"It wouldn't be right. I'm running off and leaving you shorthanded again."

"You work, we pay. It's that simple."

"Nothing is ever that simple."

"This time it is." Amy wished she didn't like Heath so much. That's what this was— she couldn't lie to herself anymore. And why bother? He was leaving. "Come in for a few minutes and warm up, before you head back."

"I'd appreciate that. It's a long walk."

"And cold." All the way up the slick steps, she wondered what she was going to say to Paige. Her older sister had been upset they'd hired a man with no references; they hadn't even asked him to fill out an application, just the paperwork required by the state and federal government.

Amy fit her key in the lock and wiggled it until it gave way enough to turn—it was tricky in the freezing weather. The bolt clicked and she opened up, grateful for the warm air fanning her face as she entered. Peace. It wrapped around her every time she came home. The pile of toys neat in the corner by the couch. The pictures of family—of her sisters, of Paige's son and dozens of Westin from the moment he was born on up.

She noticed Heath closed the door behind him, looking neither right nor left as he followed her into the kitchen. While he set the keys on the corner of the counter, she filled two cups with tap water and set them in the middle of the mounted microwave. It hummed as she extracted items from the cupboards. Aware of Heath watching her the whole while, his presence shrank the small space until it seemed there were only the two of them and the walls pressing in.

For some reason, he must have felt it, too, because he didn't look comfortable. Maybe because he was a big man and the alley kitchen was narrow. He hardly fit in the walkway between the counter and the corner of the stove. Edgy, he didn't seem to know where to look, glancing quickly from the toys to the pictures to Westin's artwork tacked on the fridge.

Maybe it was the trailer—a lot of folks looked down on them, as if they were only for poor people. But she wasn't poor. Not when she had so many blessings.

Maybe it was because she was still in her pajamas and they were more strangers than friends. She reached for the business checkbook and a pen. "Did you want to take a seat?"

"Sure."

He didn't look any more comfortable in the small chair at the little dinette set that had once been her mother's. The set was a bright Valentine's-Day-pink with metal sides and

legs. It was a very feminine-looking table—
and if that wasn't bad enough, all six-plus
feet of him barely fitted in the small chair that
was as pink as the little table.

The microwave dinged. She removed the
steaming mugs and ripped open two packets of cocoa mix. "I know, it's not sophisticated but this kind does have the little mini
marshmallows."

His jaw clamped and a muscle jumped
along his jaw.

Okay, maybe he didn't like marshmallows.
"I can scoop them out if you want."

"No, it's all right."

It didn't look all right, but she didn't say
anything more. She stirred the mix until it
dissolved and spooned the tiny marshmallows from his cup.

"You think I'm looking for a husband, don't
you? That's why you're bugging out of here
as fast as you can go. No, it's okay. I'm not
mad." She slipped the mug in front of him.

It had flowers on it and said in rainbow-
colored writing, The Best Mom Ever! with,
I Thank God for You printed beneath it.

Heath stared at it as if the cup were the single most horrible thing he'd ever seen.

"It was the only one without a chip in it. I have a six-year-old boy and no dishwasher. Being hand-washed around here is hazardous for mugs."

The color drained from his face.

Maybe it wasn't the femininity of the cup that was bothering him. If she'd been thinking, she would have remembered there was also the Bible passage on the mug. He wasn't a churchgoer. She knew how it felt to feel pressured about one's faith or lack of it. Through her own experience, it seemed God came to those who needed Him most when they needed him.

Heath surely looked as if he were a man hurting. She switched the cups and reached for a spoon to transfer the frothy marshmallows. "Maybe you wouldn't mind this one as much. It's just got a little chip."

"No, don't bother." He nudged the damaged mug back. The tendons stood out like ropes in his neck.

"Look, I can't do this." He pushed away from the table. "Keep the money. I appreciate the job, I do. I just—" he glanced around, the light draining from his eyes as he headed to the door "—can't."

She hadn't even had the chance to finish the check. Where was he going? And on foot? She grabbed the keys, for she meant for him to drive back to town. He could leave her car at the diner and she'd catch a ride to work with Rachel. It was too cold for him to walk all the way to the diner. She hated to think of him cold and alone and miserable.

What would make him bolt out of here as if he'd been set on fire?

Then she looked behind her at the wall. Westin's framed baby pictures decorated the space between the fridge and the wall. Adorable pictures of her son when he was first sitting up and learning to walk.

In those pictures, it was hard to miss his downy soft platinum hair, sparkling blue eyes and the way he was all boy. Westin at that age had a spirit as sweet as spun sugar....

Looking at those pictures, she realized exactly why Heath's heart was as lost as one of the black holes Westin was always reading about. Tears wet her cheek before she realized they were falling.

Please, Father, she prayed, *help him.*

There was no answer in the endless silence.

Chapter Nine

She found him in the snow, just standing there as if he'd gotten only that far before the pain took over. Tiny perfect crystal flakes had gathered in his dark hair and graced the breadth of his shoulders. He was such a big strong man and yet how could any one person be mighty enough to withstand the immense grief he'd known?

Sympathy moved through her as she laid a hand on his wide back. She wasn't surprised at all that he felt like steel. But she wasn't prepared for the virulent explosion of emotion, like a supernova's shock waves, that radiated from him and into her. She felt as if she could feel his soul.

Oh, Heath. She'd never known such agony; not the loss of her parents when she was young, not the desperate life in a cruel city. Nothing she'd been through compared to the pain she felt rolling through her.

It was an all-encompassing pain. And how could it be anything else? A child was infinitely precious. How well she remembered the thrill and the intense burst of love she'd felt the first time she'd held her son in her arms. She tried to imagine Heath with his son. The pride he would have felt. And more, so much more. He would have harbored every hope of happiness for his son. A joyful, carefree childhood and the chance through education or training to achieve his dreams.

She knew, too, Heath would have dreamed of spending the years to come with his boy. Of lazy summer afternoons fishing along the shady banks of a quiet river. Of loud roaring crowds and hot dogs and a perfect view of home base. Of college graduation and the pride a father took in his son growing into a fine man.

The ashes of those dreams remained, imprinted forever into Heath's soul. But otherwise, they were gone like ashes scattered in a bitter wind.

She leaned her forehead against the unyielding plane of his shoulder blade. She was barely aware of the bitter cold, accumulating snow and dissipating fog curling around them, shrouding them from the neighbors, from the street, from the world.

There were just the two of them and Heath didn't move. Except for the rise and fall of his chest and the thump of his heartbeat, he could have been cast in stone. In some ways, Amy realized, he was.

She hadn't held a man in a long time, but she simply did it without knowing why. She wrapped her arms around his waist, feeling the thick muscled feel of him, and held on. Overcome, she pressed her cheek against his back and did the only thing she could. She let him know that he wasn't alone.

And so they remained until the sun warmed the cold black mountains to the east. The first streaks of gold haloed the tiniest of snowflakes that fell like a promise over the crisp white earth. Dawn came as wide streaks of light broke free from behind the mountains.

Heath slipped from her arms, without a

word of explanation or apology. She pressed the keys to her car in his hand along with the thick fold of bills—her tip money from yesterday, since his paycheck was still half-written on her kitchen table.

He didn't say a word as he pushed the keys and money back into her palm. Pure pain twisted his face as he walked into the glare of the sunrise and disappeared from her sight.

The most beautiful mornings seemed to always follow the cruel storms.

The cheerful sun had Amy blinking against the brightness as lemony rays shot through the slats of the diner's white window blinds. She poured two cups of coffee from the first batch of brew of the day. The front door was still locked—they had four minutes to go until opening time, and she needed it.

Stifling a jaw-splitting yawn, she brought both cups of coffee to the far booth near the kitchen, where Jodi was lacing up her tennis shoes. She was bleary-eyed from working a late shift at her second job. Single moms had to do what they could to make ends meet, even if it was working late at night.

The dawn seemed unaware of their indifference. Sunshine beamed between the slats in the opened blinds and warmed the morning. Amy tried to keep her thoughts on the day ahead—Westin had a doctor's appointment this afternoon and she needed to go grocery shopping. She had to call Kelly because, with Heath gone, she was likely going to have to work a shift tonight and would need a baby-sitter.

"I suppose Paige'll be here soon on a rampage." Jodi winked as she gave the sugar canister a nudge and it slid to Amy. "She's been gone for two weeks. She'll have all kinds of energy saved up for us. I'm looking forward to it."

"Sure, because you're not related to her." Amy loved her oldest sister. Everybody did. Paige was just…used to being in charge and that had been fine when Amy was ten but now that she was twenty-five, it was a different story.

Plus, when Paige found out Heath was gone, Amy was going to get another lecture on the proper method of interviewing employees to safeguard against this kind of thing. Poor Paige, she did everything she could to protect herself, to keep bad things from happening. She tried so hard, but, as far as Amy saw, there wasn't much to be done about preventing some things.

Just like with Heath. Amy dumped plenty of sugar into her coffee and stirred, watching the dark liquid, remembering how Heath had made her hot chocolate last night. Odd, she couldn't remember the last time a man had made her anything at all—maybe if she could remember her father, but she couldn't. The everyday minutia of that happy life had blurred with time. She couldn't draw his face in her memory anymore. And as for Westin's father, well, he was more the kind who demanded to be waited on.

Remembering how lost Heath had seemed, shrouded by fog, blanketed by snow, she hoped that wherever he was, he'd found peace. Surely God took special care of lost souls, saved or not. She'd always found great comfort that in spite of the dark, lonely time in Seattle when she'd turned her back on her faith, God was watching out for her regardless.

Not that she would have recognized it at the time, but she was wiser now. She had faith that Heath wasn't alone—not truly.

Across the empty main street a freight

train rumbled along the tracks, the boxcars hiding the green park and meadows as they rolled endlessly on. Amy sipped her coffee, savoring the peace, and tried again not to think about Heath. Tried not to wonder where he was. Had he found a motel to catch a few hours sleep before driving on?

Finally, the caboose capped the end of the long procession and, as the train disappeared from sight, the town fell silent and motionless. Not even the white-faced Herefords in the field behind the tracks moved. Nor did the thickets of buttercups and dandelions. If she squinted, she could see the brand-new roofs of homes in the subdivision beyond that. All was still there, too.

Peace. Amy absorbed it as she sipped her coffee.

"There's Mr. Brisbane's truck." Jodi swigged back the last of her coffee. "Time to get to work."

Amy took her cup with her, leaving Jodi to flip around the open sign and unlock the front door. It was a few minutes before six, but for the morning group, it didn't matter. They were more family than customers anyway.

Amy just wished she wasn't so beat. Exhaustion weighed her down, and she felt as though she was moving in slow motion as she pushed through the swinging doors into the kitchen. She was on the grill for the breakfast shift, so her thoughts were already turning to putting on extra bacon for Mr. Winkler and maple sausage for Mr. Brisbane. She was thinking ahead to their orders—she needed to open a new can of jalapeños—so when she saw the hulking man at the grill, she didn't recognize him. Adrenaline shot into her blood. *Oh, no, more trouble...*

No, it was Heath. He was at the grill. He was starting to cook.

What was he doing here? She hadn't spotted his pickup in the back lot when she'd arrived. She hadn't heard him come in, but it really was him. He didn't look up as he slapped thick strips of bacon onto the grill. The sizzle and snap filled the long stretch of silence as her thoughts switched tracks and she realized that he was real and no dream.

"'Mornin'." Abrupt, cold as glacial ice, he kept his back firmly turned. He finished with the bacon and began setting links of sausage on the grill.

He'd been busy while she'd been in the

dining room drinking coffee. Bread stood in the industrial-sized toaster ready to be put down. The pancake batter was mixed, and he'd already put a pan of muffins in the oven. Incredible.

"Good morning." Amy opened the fridge and pulled out a big batch of cinnamon rolls, iced and fresh and ready to be heated. "I wasn't expecting you."

Heath remained silent and stiff. A stone statue couldn't have been less interactive.

He stared through the order-up counter into the dining room while he worked, as if he were very interested in Jodi's conversation with Bob Brisbane about the snow that had come and gone, and the damage to the front windows.

The kitchen seemed silent in contrast. Way too silent. Questions rushed to the tip of her tongue, but she didn't ask them. She didn't know why Heath had returned, but she sensed if she asked him about it, then he'd be gone for good. So she reset the oven, careful not to get too close while she rescued the perfectly baked muffins.

"Sorry I'm late."

He didn't sound sorry, he sounded empty. "It was just a few minutes. Don't worry about it."

"It won't happen again."

"Okay."

He was treating her as if their earlier emotional intimacy had never happened. She could still feel the deepest of sorrow clinging to him. And if he needed distance to cope, she could give him that. It wasn't as if there could be more anyway. She wasn't looking for love—that was absolutely out of the question. Maybe they would wind up as friends, and a girl could never have too many of those blessings.

Heath looked like someone who could use a friend, too. "Did you get any sleep?"

"I didn't, but that's not unusual." She loaded the industrial-sized toaster as the door jangled, announcing another customer. "You?"

He shook his head instead of answering and turned his back. His message was clear. The conversation, such as it was, was over.

The deputy shouldered through the threshold, uniformed, his hat in hand. He caught her gaze, nodded once as if he wanted to speak with her when she got the chance, and took a table near the back.

Since Heath looked purposefully busy, keeping his back rigid, his head turned, it wasn't hard to figure out there was no point trying to help out in the kitchen. He could handle it, and he clearly wasn't comfortable around her, so she let him be. On her way past the coffee station, she snatched the carafe and the back of her neck tingled. She knew Heath was watching her, although when she looked up, his attention was on his work.

It was likely to be a busy morning, she thought as she squinted at the sun-bright windows. Several pickups and cars were starting to fill the parking slots outside. Jodi was busy with the regulars, so Amy grabbed a folded newspaper and headed straight for Frank's table.

She didn't ask if he wanted coffee, he always wanted coffee, so she simply turned over the cup in its saucer and filled it with the steaming brew. "I don't know if I thanked you enough for all you did last night."

"It's my job, you know that. I was glad I was able to help out."

"It wasn't your job to stay after those men were arrested. Or to carry plywood and nail it up, and nothing you say is going to convince me otherwise." She handed him a menu. "Will those guys be out on bail anytime soon?"

"The bail bondsman wouldn't cover them, so they're staying until their hearing on Monday morning. Maybe a stint in lock-up will give them time to do a little thinking, and they'll straighten up."

"I hope so, for everyone's sake." At least she didn't have to worry about any more retribution, at least for now. She trusted the local law enforcement to keep an eye on the situation. Just think, if both the deputy and the sheriff hadn't been so willing to hop out of bed in the middle of the night, how much more damage would those two drunks have done?

Amy shuddered at the thought. "Do you need some time, or do you know what you want?"

"I already have a hankering for your eggs Benedict." He scanned the listings. "You wouldn't be able to make that a combination meal for me, would you?"

"For you, anything." She took back the menu, scribbling on the ticket as she went and underlining, Generous Portions, because she owed Frank, too.

"Order in." She clipped the ticket to the wheel, but Heath ignored her as he sprinkled cheese into the open face of a cooking omelet.

It was pretty clear this was how it was going to be between them. As the morning passed in a flurry of activity, Heath didn't look at her once. He spoke to her only when absolutely necessary for the job.

While she was disappointed, if that's what he needed, then fine. Thinking about what he'd lost, she gave deep thanks for her son. The best gift she'd ever been given. She couldn't let her mind roll forward to imagine losing Westin—no, she couldn't *think* about it. She just couldn't.

But for what Heath had suffered, he had her respect. She didn't question him. She didn't try to talk to him more than necessary. Paige came in, all aflurry, bent on calling every last glass man in the phone book to get the best price. She was a good business-woman, but Amy's heart was no longer in the loss of a window or the thoughtless retribu-tion of two sorry men who'd been fired from the mill, as Frank had told her on his way out the door.

She might have a ten-year-old car and a job that wasn't fancy, exciting or impressive, but she could provide for her son. She lived modestly and she didn't have a high-school diploma. Some people might not think she had a lot, but they would be wrong. She had everything. Everything that mattered.

Although the morning was busy, she made sure she found time to give Paige a hug, call her son before Rachel took him to school, and thank God for the blessings in her life.

Rachel poked her head around the corner and into the small space where Amy was popping aspirin for her headache. "Is the coast clear?"

"It's clear. Paige went to the bank." Amy tipped back her head and swallowed. The aspirin stuck in her throat, and the acrid bitter taste filled her mouth. She washed it down with her lukewarm soda—it wasn't much help. "It's almost time for me to go pick Westin up from school. I've almost got these orders done."

"The ones I was supposed to do?" Rachel brightened like the first star on a clear summer's night. "Oh, Amy. I love you, I love you, I love you. Oh, you know how I hate doing paperwork."

"That's what you get for promising to buy out Paige's share of the restaurant next year."

"I know." Rachel glanced heavenward. "I'm going to need some help with God on that one, but I'll get the hang of crunching numbers. Really, I will."

"Or you'll get me to do it." With a wink, Amy pushed away from the desk, taking her soda with her. "I'm gladly relinquishing the paperwork to you. I'll keep my cell on if you have a question. I think I did everything right, but you never know."

"Oh, I owe ya! Thanks." Rachel lowered her voice. "Is Heath still working out as well?"

"He handled the breakfast and lunch crowd like a pro. We couldn't have found anyone better."

"Oh, I'm so glad. He's heaven-sent, I have a feeling about it." Rachel backed out of the way, since the built-in desk was at the back of the closet-office and there wasn't a lot of room to turn around in the narrow space. "Oh, and you're out of sugar. I added it to the bottom of your grocery list, though."

"You're a sweetie. Thanks." Amy grabbed her purse and caught sight of Heath putting the last of the dishes in the dishwasher. He snapped his head back to his work, as if he'd been listening, or at least watching for her.

A muscle tensed along his jaw before he turned completely away.

Amy looked at the long lean line of his iron-hard shoulders and remembered how cold his back had felt against her cheek. She left without a word, without even saying goodbye, figuring he wanted it that way. Rachel had to be right—Heath was a blessing, and she prayed hard, hoping he could stay on. But if he couldn't take being around children, and a lot of children came to the diner, then she'd understand.

The screen-door hinges squeaked, but it was a pleasant sound as she stepped out into the beautiful day. The fragrance of the lilacs carried on the wind, and she breathed deep. The warm fresh air invigorated her, at least a little. It was hard to believe last night had been so bleak, but a few puddles remained as a reminder and she stepped around them.

It was a spring day like so many that had come before. Like so many that would follow today. But the moment seemed brighter, accented by the chirp of birds and the meow of a cat enjoying the shelter beneath her car. As she knelt to shoo it gently away, apple blossoms fluttered along the warm rays of the sun.

As tired as she was, she felt as if she'd picked up a second wind. The thought of spending the afternoon with her son picked up her spirits. She tossed her purse on the sun-warmed seat, rolled down her window and dug her keys out of her hip pocket.

"Amy?"

Heath stood in the shade of the building, blending very neatly with the shadows in the dark jeans and T-shirt he wore. His hands were jammed into his pockets, his arms muscular and his frame lean. He looked ready for a fight.

Had he come to explain himself? Or to give his two-weeks' notice? Either way, she saw a man struggling. A man alone.

She glanced at her wristwatch. "I have a few minutes before school lets out. What do you need?"

"To apologize." He ambled forward, tentatively, into the scorching kiss of the afternoon sun.

"For what?"

Somewhere down the street a dog barked. She waited as he came closer. Exhaustion had dug harsh lines into his noble face. He walked slowly, and it was as if all the life inside him had gone out. "For walking away from you like that. It was rude."

"I think I understand."

His head rolled forward and he gasped for breath, as if she'd struck him. But it was from the truth of his past, the fresh mention of what he'd lost.

If she were in his shoes, she could never speak of such a loss. And while she had so many questions, there were so many things she didn't know about him and what had happened to him. How old had his son been? Had his marriage crumbled beneath the strain of a child's death? What greater loss or hardship could there be in a marriage? She didn't ask because he was in enough pain, so she waited, wondering what he would volunteer.

"I had my duffel packed. You know that. I had made up my mind to leave. But this morning when I was walking back here, the snow started to melt. It was a strange thing, to see snow on the ground and flowers blooming up through it."

"If you've been in Montana as long as I have, it's not so strange. Wait until it's the middle of July. It's weird to cancel a Fourth of July picnic because of a blizzard."

Her attempt at humor at least eased the depth of the lines dug around his severe mouth. "I got to thinking. You and your sisters are having some trouble, and I helped out some."

"Yes, and we'll always be grateful to you."

"I haven't made a difference to anyone in a long while." He stared hard at a small puddle on the blacktop between them.

She waited while the minutes ticked by and a dog started barking down the street and Heath struggled to find the right words. The dog barked on and on until someone called out, "Would you shut up!" and he did.

Then there was only the hush of the wind between them.

He took a ragged breath, betraying all that it cost him to explain. "I'm grateful to feel useful again. I've been wandering for so long—ever since the funeral. Once they were gone, I roamed from one town to the next because I had…nothing."

Once they were gone. Amy's heart dropped, realizing he'd lost not only his son.

"I can't make any promises, but I need to stay for now."

She read the bleak truth in him. "Of course. Rachel and I both think you're a godsend. I know you're not a believer—"

"I am, I'm just…lost."

"No, you're never lost."

His throat worked. He stared up at the trees where cheerful leaves whispered and danced. The dog down the street started barking again.

"There is one more thing. A favor you can do for me." He withdrew his right hand from his jeans pocket and there, on his palm, was a nine-volt battery. "You have a son. Put this in your smoke detector. Do it the minute you walk through the door. Don't put it off."

The battery was warm from his body heat. She stared at it, wondering how he knew that she'd taken the old one out last week because it had been beeping at 2:46 a.m. There hadn't been a new one left in the junk drawer to put in its place.

Oh. Realization washed over her with a new horror. He was already walking away, part of the shadows and hard to see through her tears.

Chapter Ten

Memories had followed him to sleep, rearing up in his nightmares until he woke for the fourth time in a cold sweat, shouting his son's name. The rasping heave of his breathing sounded loud in the small bedroom where the curtains billowed at the open window, letting in the ghostly silvered light of a half moon.

With the echoes of his son's name dissipating like smoke, Heath flung off the sheet and raked his hand through his wet hair. The pure golden light of first dawn blasted against the undersides of the pull-down blinds that were wobbling in place over the open window. The sunshine bled through the billowing sheers and onto the foot of his bed.

At least the night was over, he could be glad for that, even if he was awake at 4:55 a.m. He lay there for a while, listening to the cheerful birds and a train's low keening whistle and the rumbling as it chugged along. The dog that had been barking yesterday let out a few yelps and fell silent.

He gave the old blind a good yank and it only rolled halfway up. It annoyed him, but when he sat back on the edge of the bed, he could see the peaceful river valley. It shone so green and beautiful, a perfect carpet at the feet of the great mountains ringing the low lush valley. The breeze felt cool on his face, and it was almost as if he could forget.

It was a world apart here. He could pretend that Portland didn't exist. The way the enormous mountains marched like giants in all directions, it seemed as if nothing else could possibly be on the other side of their amazing rugged peaks. He wanted to believe that the quiet harmony of this place was a world apart from the more desperate one he'd been running from. He was so weary.

So infinitely weary.

As for Amy McKaslin, she knew the unspeakable truth. The look on her face after he'd given her the battery, when realization hit, said it all. He'd watched her realize the horrible truth he could not say. She should have hated him, but no, not Amy. She was a mom—it was his guess that little Westin was her very world. She'd understood.

But no one could truly comprehend the grief and guilt until they'd walked this path.

He wished no other parent ever had to.

He'd tried to work for a while, tried to put all his sorrow and rage and desperation to good use. He'd worked long hard hours in the ER and he'd made a difference, but there was still death and loss, illness and injury. People still died.

The last straw had been working alongside the pediatric specialist for an hour trying to save a seven-month-old girl. The infant had been symptom-free after a car accident, for she'd been safely buckled in her infant car seat and had then presented that afternoon with shocky symptoms. Heath heard the baby's cry, realized something was wrong, had chewed out the admittance nurse and ordered the young mother and her baby into the nearest available trauma room.

He put in a call to the peds surgeon, but it

was too late. Massive internal bleeding. He'd done everything, even prayed to a God he knew good and well didn't protect innocent children.

He'd broken down afterward. No procedure had been spared, and they had all worked so hard for the little red-haired girl and her silently crying mother. Even the mother comforted him, he'd taken it so hard.

He'd sat in the corner and the grief he'd been holding back flooded him like a tidal wave crashing to shore and there had been no recovering. It had been six weeks since the fire. Five and a half weeks since the funeral. All because he'd been too busy, too tired, too forgetful to buy a three-dollar battery.

He'd never be all right again—never. There would be no peace, no forgiveness, no anything. He didn't want there to be. He didn't deserve it. He'd failed the two people who mattered more to him than anything. He didn't deserve the right to anything.

But now, after all these months, he was soul-weary. Tired of wandering. He was a man who liked roots, who missed the bonds of family and friends and colleagues and patients. He deserved the harsh sting of loneliness. Not that he'd ever settle down or try to live a normal life, but it sure felt nice to think about resting here for a while. He could help out the McKaslin sisters, salute the deputy when they crossed paths, breathe in the serenity of this place and just exist without a past, without a future.

After he shaved and showered, he popped a cup of water into the microwave for instant coffee, then heard a car pull to a stop in the back lot. Curious, he ambled around to the living room, where the old blinds snapped up with an echoing twang and down below was a spotless forest-green SUV.

It wasn't more lowlifes looking for trouble, just the oldest sister. The serious one. With dark glasses shading her eyes, her brown hair tight in a ponytail, she walked soundlessly across the parking lot. She carried a bunch of ledgers in one arm. Remembering Amy and Rachel's discussion about keeping the books for Paige almost made him smile.

Yeah, they looked like a real nice family. It wasn't a bad thing, helping them out.

It was early, but he stirred up the coffee and slurped it down as he maneuvered the steps. Paige had left the back door wide open, guarded only by the unlocked screen.

He didn't want to startle her, so he knocked before he opened up. "Hello?"

"Oh, hi. Heath, isn't it?" Paige had the look of a woman who had too much to do in too little time. She was taller than Amy and Rachel, and not as vibrant. There was a quiet steel in her he immediately respected. She ran a good restaurant and, as far as he could tell, she managed the extended family, too. "Come on in, although you're early. I just put some coffee on…oh, that isn't that old stale instant stuff? It's got to be years and years old."

"You don't rent the apartment often?"

"No, it got to be too much to deal with. One kind of trouble after another, and to tell you the truth, I have as much of that as I can handle right now." She smiled to soften her words and gave a self-conscious shrug. "You might as well sit down and enjoy some coffee. I've got some baked goods still out in my Jeep."

"I can get 'em for you if you want."

"Wow, that would be great." Relief and appreciation lit her eyes that looked so tired. "I didn't lock it."

Working here might require more involvement on a personal level than he was used to, but he liked feeling useful. He almost recognized the man he used to be.

The morning light felt gentle, and already the air was beginning to warm. He lifted the back hatch of the SUV and was instantly assaulted by the wave of cinnamon and sweetness and doughnut goodness. The delicious aroma distracted him, so he didn't notice her until it was almost too late.

Amy McKaslin in a pair of navy shorts and a matching T-shirt, her hair drawn back, speed-walking along the alley. She looked for a moment as though she regretted that she'd been spotted. As if resigned, she diverted from the alley and cut between the lilacs to the parking lot. She was breathing heavily and sweat glistened on her brow.

"You caught me. I'm trying to keep to a work-out program, but it's impossible with my schedule. I haven't walked for about three weeks and I'm ready to keel over."

"I could save you with a cinnamon roll."

"No, then I'd have to walk even more."

Heath hadn't thought he would be glad to see her, but he was. She'd breached the distance he kept everyone at, and he wasn't bothered by it. He wasn't sure if that was a good sign or a bad one. "Are you working this morning?"

"Nope. I gotta get back to my little boy. It's almost time for him to get up. I've got Mrs. Nash, she's next door, keeping an eye on him for me. Ooh, huckleberry coffeecake. That's absolutely incredible. You should sneak a piece before the customers start arriving, because it goes fast. I've gotta get going. Bye!"

She was hurrying away from him, he could see it. What had happened stood between them. He wanted to ask her if she'd taken his advice and changed the battery in her smoke detector, but he couldn't say the words. If he asked, then it would be too close to talking about what happened, and he just couldn't say the words.

So he watched her hurry off, her long tanned legs stretching and bunching, her muscles rippling, her ponytail flickering back in her wake. Swept by sunlight, she disappeared around the shadows from the tall maples at the block's end. The same dog started barking until someone yelled at it to stop.

It was five-thirty; a train rolled through

clanging and clattering and tooting so loudly he swore the earth beneath his feet rumbled. There was a comforting rhythm to a day starting out here, at the diner. He set the baked goods on the counter, put a big square of huckleberry coffeccake on a plate, grabbed a fork and headed for the coffee station.

Paige had already poured her cup, so he did his own and took the closest booth by the windows. He set down his food and saw the teenager on a motorcycle coming to an idling stop at the curb out front. He tossed a half dozen rolled newspapers onto the front mat and drove off with the rough rumbling sound of a small motorcycle in need of a muffler.

Heath hopped outside, noticing the handle on the door could use some tightening. Then he gathered up the papers, set all but one on the top of the counter by the till and unwound the rubber band from the last roll. The crisp newsprint splashed across the front page was about the upcoming Founder's Day jubilee.

Sipping his coffee, he began reading the local news. As he read, he recognized several of the names in the articles or in the letters to the editor section. It was odd to live in a place and feel a part of it again.

The deputy dropped by a few minutes early, and Jodi came rushing in behind him, out of breath. Mr. Brisbane rolled to a stop at the curb in his grass-green classic pickup.

It was time to go to work.

Heath knew the exact moment when she walked in the diner. It was as if a warm summer's dawn had touched the dark places in his soul.

He finished dressing the sandwiches for table four and didn't even need to turn around. He could feel the radiance of her, becoming more brilliant as she moved closer. The screen door slapping shut, her sneakers squeaking on the freshly cleaned tile and the thump of her purse landing on the corner shelf were all clues.

Clues he didn't need. His heart turned toward her the way a flower does toward the light, and he knew, would have known even if he had been rendered deaf and blind, that she was coming to stand beside him.

"Hey, I'm ready to go. A few minutes late—"

Paige scowled from the other side of the

order-up window. "A few minutes? I'm docking your pay."

"Ha! I was trying to make those calls from home while I finished up some laundry. You know, the calls to the glass-replacement people?"

"Sorry. I'm still docking you." A ghost of a smile was the only hint that Paige was teasing.

Amy, however, was not as deadpan. "Okay, then I'll just go back home and let you take over for Heath."

Heath's head was spinning; he was trying to make sense of the growing brightness within him. The luster he felt came from her, from Amy, there was no doubt about it. She made some comment to her sister, something that he couldn't follow, his brain couldn't seem to focus on that. But he was aware of her moving away, gliding like a pianist's scale—one note flowed into the next, trilling away like music and rolling back again.

The women were talking, familiar and companionable with one another. Families were like that. He'd been close to his sister, teasing her gently just to see her smile. Family ties, they were a fine thing.

And while he'd missed the late-night long-distance calls and the quick e-mails sent when his parents or his sister had had time enough, it wasn't the loneliness that made him keenly aware of Amy standing beside him, making him tingle like electrical feeders siphoning up from the ground in a lightning storm.

No, this wasn't about the long stretch of loneliness or the need for a soft place to rest, just for a moment. This stirring within him was powerful enough to rock his soul.

He couldn't force his gaze away from her. Exhaustion marked her. She didn't look as if she'd caught up on much missed sleep last night. The bruises beneath her eyes were a dark purple. He remembered her comment from yesterday, how getting little sleep was not out of the ordinary for her.

As she wet and soaped her hands in the sink, he wondered what kept her awake at night. The past? Her responsibilities?

"My car is making this horrible noise and you know there goes another six hundred dollars." Amy rinsed, grabbed a paper towel and dried, still talking to her oldest sister, still unaware that he was watching her and pretending not to.

Car trouble? He had noticed the clutch felt a little soft when he'd driven it, but there was no noise. He didn't need to see the worry on Amy's face or how modestly she lived to know a car repair bill would be a hardship.

"Didn't you just get the last thing paid off?"

"Yeah, the transmission." Amy wadded up the paper towel and tossed it into the trash.

He heaped fries on the plates, laid down the orange sections for garnish and slipped the last orders of his shift on the hand-off window. Paige, always efficient, circled around to serve the sandwiches.

"I guess it's your turn to go home." Amy busily tied on her flowered apron and began hauling out bowls, measuring cups and spoons. "Before you go, can I make you something to eat?"

He saw the big round blue of her eyes watching him, innocently unaware that he *felt*. "No, I'd better get out of here."

She had no idea how true that was. It was as if he'd stepped on a land mine and he knew if he so much as breathed wrong, the charge would go off.

"Okay. Are you working the late shift tonight?"

"No. I told Paige I'd best be here late, so none of the women are here alone. Considering what happened. But she said she'd be fine."

"That's decent of you."

That's me, he wanted to say, decent to the core. But it wasn't true. If he were decent, then he wouldn't allow any feelings for her into his heart. He had no right, not to anything. Not to a future or happiness or the chance to love again. He'd failed to keep his loved ones safe.

He'd failed them.

Amy knew, and she didn't treat him with hate or accusation. When he'd handed her the battery yesterday, her face had crumpled with sadness. She was a compassionate woman, she gave people the benefit of the doubt. Wild birds weren't scared of her, and she was like spring come to his frozen tundra heart.

"What kind of noise is your car making?" He couldn't believe he'd said it.

Neither could she because she looked up from pouring teriyaki marinade into a big bowl and she studied at him with wonder. "Well, why am I surprised? Let me guess. You've been a mechanic, too."

"Not a journeyman or anything, but I worked at one of those quick lube places. I did brakes, tune-ups and radiators."

"What do you know about carburetors?"

"They can be expensive to replace."

"Great. That's just what I know about them, too." Amy capped the bulky industrial-sized bottle of marinade and gazed across the distance between them, a few feet, and yet it felt as wide as the Pacific Ocean.

She unwrapped fresh chicken filets and slipped them into the bowl, covered them well with the marinade, clipped on the top and left them in the refrigerator beside a bowl with the exact same thing in it. It was good to keep her hands busy so she wouldn't be tempted to take Heath up on his generous offer.

She did the same with the perfect stack of petite filet mignon the butcher had delivered fresh and wrapped. She tenderized the meat, aerated it, sprinkled the family's secret steak flavoring and covered the dish. After fitting it into the crammed fridge, she turned around and there was Heath, reaching for the notebook to sign out.

"Excuse me." She moved a step back.

He didn't.

"Come by here for dinner tonight, okay?" she asked, talking to fill the silence falling between them. To cover the sound of the rushing in her ears and the fast tinny beat of her heart. "Come in the back, let them know what you want. That's the rule for our employees."

When he didn't answer, her brows creased. As if frustrated with him, she shook her head, scattering stray gold wisps of her hair that fell into her eyes. She shut the refrigerator door and blew the bangs out of the way.

Try to act normal, he coached himself. Act like nothing is happening.

Except it was.

He wanted to smooth the wayward strands away from her face. He wanted to trail his fingertips across the soft curve of her cheek to know if her creamy skin was as soft as it looked. He wanted to brush tiny kisses along the barely noticeable freckles sprinkled across her nose and cheeks.

It was an impulse, this deep yearning to take care of her and to care for her. It scared him. Suddenly the walls felt as if they were inching in and he was caged. Out—he wanted outside. Trying to keep a lid on his panic, he moved casually but as quickly as he could, and spotted the full garbage can by the back door.

It was the perfect excuse to leave. He tied off the sack, grabbed his baseball cap and tore outside into the building heat of the midday sun. The bright round disc was nearly straight overhead and his shadow was small as he marched over it, walking fast and far, wanting peace. And if he couldn't have those, than he'd settle for being numb again. His heart hurt like an arm or leg long unused, crying out to protest the stretch and bend of weakened muscle.

Heath swore the chambers of his heart were expanding, ready to explode like a bomb. He tossed the heavy bag into the big green Dumpster and dragged in deep, cutting breaths. The hot breeze and the wide-open space of the back parking lot made some of that edgy panicky feeling fade.

The thing was, he didn't want to care. Caring came hand in hand with vulnerability. Vulnerability brought inevitable loss. He was better off alone because caring about people only led to hurt. There was no other way about it.

"Heath?"

Amy stood on the threshold, the dim kitchen behind her, and the bright wash of spring before. She was as vivid as the day— her golden hair, creamy skin, soft pink T-shirt, ruffled calico apron. She shaded her eyes with one slender hand. "Are you okay?"

"Yeah, sure." It was a lie, they both knew it.

Answering her honestly would only lead to talking, and talking to confessing and that's what he'd done. Look at what trusting some-one led to. She'd come to ask how he was be-cause she cared. She remained standing in the hot sun, waiting for him to come closer.

No. This was as far as his involvement went. He tugged the bill of his cap low, as if to keep the sun out of his eyes, but it was so that she couldn't see in.

Without a word, he pivoted on his heel and followed the wind as far away from her as he could get.

Chapter Eleven

"I think we're going to stay slow," Paige said as she unpacked canned goods from the earlier, midmorning delivery. "The noon hour is past, and we didn't have much of a rush. Why don't you pack that sandwich to go, if you'd rather. I'll stay and handle all this. I know you put in way too many hours while I was gone."

Amy wrapped the sandwich good and tight and slipped it into a plastic bag. She sealed the zipper lock and looked around for a suitable size to-go bag. She chose the smaller size and snapped it open beside the meal she'd made for herself.

"Rachel and I tried, but there's no filling your shoes."

"Yeah, yeah. Compliments will get you everywhere. Oh, I saved a few brownies for you to take home. I know they're Westin's favorites."

"That will make my little boy smile."

"Just trying to keep my nephew happy." Paige took time to smile before she hauled the heavy box into the storage closet. "Go home. Enjoy some time off."

"I will. I've got books to return and a house to clean." If she hurried, she'd be done in time to pick up Westin from school. "Oh, I found out the time for his graduation on Friday. It's two o'clock in the gym."

"I'll be there with the video recorder. Oh, I bet I can get Jodi to stay a little longer to cover me." Paige abandoned her restocking to dart over to the little office. "I'll write it on the calendar so I don't forget to ask her."

She had no sooner started to scribble than the phone rang. "I'll get it. Go. Get out of here while you can!"

Amy filled two containers of pasta salad, wrapped up the last of the brownies and decided on two cans of iced tea. Since her sister was still on the phone, Amy grabbed up the stuffed to-go bags, one in each arm and darted out into the brilliant May sunshine.

She heard the window air conditioner rattling at full speed, so she dared to climb the stairs and knock on the door. No answer. She knew he was in there. The air conditioner was loud, so she gave him the benefit of the doubt and knocked louder.

Nothing.

Okay, that was a clue. He was home. He clearly wasn't going to answer the door. Yep, maybe that was her answer. He'd seemed upset, really upset. First distant, then friendly enough and then angry, at least she *thought* he was angry. After she'd gone and talked on and on about her car troubles.

All he had ever done since practically the moment he walked into the diner for a meal was to help her and her sisters. He'd defended them, he'd worked for them, he'd scared off vandals and he must be feeling as if the requests never stopped.

At least, she thought that was the issue. She'd never been good at figuring men out. Who knew what they wanted or needed and why they acted the way they did. It was probably because she couldn't really remember her dad. She had certain memories, sure, but she couldn't recall the experience of having him in her life. Only the absence that came with his passing.

No, she was terrible when it came to figuring out men. She'd failed miserably with Westin's father, but then, she'd been nineteen, so very young. She'd kept a wide berth from men since. She served coffee and meals and made polite conversation with men every day in the diner, but that was different.

But Heath…no, she didn't know what to do with him.

Looking back, Amy remembered that John had called from the hardware store about halfway through the lunch rush. While she'd busily fried up barbecue burger specials and rolled up house club wraps and filled big bowls with taco and chef salads, she'd listened to Paige down the narrow hallway at the desk. Apparently John had found replacement windows at cost, and he'd said Heath had volunteered to install them.

Heath. She couldn't get away from thinking about him. Not even though she tried. Paige had gone on about what a great find Heath Murdock was between serving orders and waiting tables. Amy had shaken her head, tossing a teriyaki chicken filet on the grill.

She knew so little about him. Where he'd grown up, all the things he must have done for a living, how long he had been drifting. What were his favorite foods? Where had he learned to make hot chocolate like that?

What she knew for sure, as she stood now on the hot outdoor staircase, was that his heart was lost. His hopes decimated. His future only ashes from the past. She knew exactly how hard it was to look back with regrets—huge, devastating regrets. She'd been an impulsive teenager who thought she knew everything. She'd ran headfirst into the realities of life. But she wasn't alone. She'd had a family to return to, a job, a home and the chance to start over.

It wasn't pity she felt for him. It was recognition. There was a time when she'd felt as if her life was nothing more than cold ashes slipping through her fingers. A dark cloud settled on her soul simply remembering that desolation. She knew what it felt like to have no hope. To have been knocked so thoroughly to the ground it seemed impossible to climb back up onto your knees and stand.

No one she trusted understood the bleak depression that had nearly choked her when she'd returned, broken and humiliated. Sure, her family had known hardship, and they certainly weren't living a carefree and luxurious life, but not even Rachel and Paige could know what it felt like to look ahead and see nothing but a dark endless void where a future was supposed to be.

Amy sighed, wondering if she should knock one more time. Heath still hadn't opened his apartment door. Was he in there, hoping she'd go away? Was he sorry she'd figured out what had happened to him?

If anyone had known what had really happened to her in Seattle, she didn't think she could stand it. That person wouldn't look at her the same way again, not without remembering.

Maybe it was like that for Heath. He didn't want to remember.

The Lord must be walking with him every second of the day. How else could Heath have kept on living? He probably wouldn't admit to it and he probably couldn't see it, but no one could survive immense sorrow without grace.

Amy set the bag lunch she'd packed for him on the top step, knocked again and headed down. Hugging her own lunch close, she thought of her blessings. Every single one of them sweetened her life like lilacs on the breeze. Tears burned in her eyes for the man upstairs. God had brought him into their diner for a reason. He had kept him here for that reason.

Is there something I should be doing, Father? Or am I to let him be? Surely Heath needed respite from his drifting. Maybe that's why he was here. To strengthen before moving on. She didn't know, but she would do that all she could.

She was almost to the bottom of the stairs when the old, weatherbeaten door scraped against the frame as it opened.

"Amy?"

He looked as if she'd woken him from a nap, and instantly she felt contrite. His hair was disheveled, a dark mop of tousled locks that made her fingers tingle. She'd never had the longing to run her fingertips through a man's hair before. With him towering over her in a wrinkled T-shirt and a crease mark from a pillow against his jawline, he looked adorable. All six-feet-plus of him, so rugged and tough, and she warmed deep inside. A new part of her soul felt as if it had winked on, like the first star in a calm summer sky.

She shook the image out of her head. There were so many extremely good reasons why she needed to rein in her growing affection for the man. But not her regard. He'd done so much good in so short a time. "I know you didn't get lunch at the diner, so I fixed a sandwich for you. I guessed and made roast beef with swiss and spicy mustard."

"Perfect." He raked his hand through his hair, making every strand stick straight up.

Even more attractive, but not in a cute way. In a way that made her wish—even when she knew better. "I tossed in a few other goodies too, chips and salad and dessert. If you're not hungry now, it'll keep in the fridge for later."

"That was pretty thoughtful of you. Say, is there a bookstore around here?"

"Not unless you're in the mood to drive to Bozeman. The Shop Mart has a book section."

"A pretty small section. I already checked it out."

"That reminds me. There's the county library on the other side of the tracks. Near the grade school."

"It's been my experience libraries only let out books to permanent town citizens. I had a library card in Portland. I read all the time. But not since I left." He shrugged one granite shoulder. "I'll survive. Thanks for the lunch."

"My pleasure."

He'd lived in Portland. Oregon? Or Maine? It was all she could think while time suspended and the twick-twick-twick of the neighbor's sprinkler faded to silence. The brilliant greens of the trees and the stunning blue of the sky and the purple of lilac cones bled their colors until the world around her was gray and Heath was all she could see.

She gasped as a strange sensation moved through her. It was as if he'd cast a fishing line, a hook had sunk deep into her heart and he'd begun to reel her in.

"I have an idea," she found herself saying. "I'll tell the librarian to add you to my account. That way you can check out books. I'd offer to do it for you, but I'm sure I can get Mrs. Pendleton to bend the rules."

"Wow, that'd be great of you."

"We've trusted you to cook for our customers, I think you're reliable enough for a library card. Besides, now I get to do something for you. Something that matters."

She glowed like her own light source, Heath realized. Maybe she didn't know it, he'd rarely seen the like. All brightness and kindness and all that was wholesome in this world. Everything that he'd stopped believing in, had pushed away from and denied.

He couldn't speak. His hand found the railing and his grip closed around the worn smooth wood. She'd known what he'd done and look at her, trusting him enough to be responsible with library books. When the truth was, the truth she couldn't see and he couldn't speak of, was that he'd been irresponsible with the greatest of God's blessings. Shame filled him like cooling lead and he could feel it move through him, hardening his spirit and his heart.

"Oh, I'm going there now," Amy called as naturally as if she were speaking to one of her sisters. "Did you want a ride?"

He managed one shake of his head. That was all.

"Okay. Make sure you ask for Mrs. Pendleton, then."

He kept staring at her.

Okay, time to go. She took one step and it felt as if the hook in her heart dug deeper.

She laid a hand on her chest and didn't know what to think. She left him standing above, so still it didn't look as if he breathed. As she dug her keys out of her jeans pocket, she wondered why it felt as if she were leaving a vital part of herself behind.

She was fine. Just the same as always. Nothing had changed in her, right? She started the engine, cringed at the horrible knocking clanging sound and put the car in gear.

All the way across the railroad tracks and the few blocks to the new brick library on a tree-lined corner, she felt the tug of that hook. Felt a powerful bond she did not want.

It was a bond she did not need.

Her car was in the shady parking lot of the modest, single-story library across from the elementary school. The streets were quiet, the students presumably tucked away inside the building, learning great things.

Forcing his attention toward Amy McKaslin's car, he didn't have to think about the empty playground, which would probably soon be full of kids running and shouting and laughing, just glad to be free. It was strange, he'd cut himself off for so long, he'd forgotten that people lived in tidy little homes that lined tree-shaded streets. Moms would come to pick up their little ones, or to meet them at the bus stop. Kids would come running with artwork and demerit notes, eager for a snack before dashing outside to play.

He almost kept going, because the library building was compact and it would be hard not to bump into Amy, since she was in there. He wasn't ready to see her. The truth was, he wanted to see her. Even if it was a bad decision. Even if there was a powerful, unexplained bond between them. So he chose a parking spot close to the exit, hopped out and locked up.

As he strolled toward the double glass entrance doors, a woman somewhere in her forties passing him gave him a nod. It felt odd, because for so long he'd been as good as invisible.

The interior of the library was cool and

crisp and smelled of paper, binding glue, leather and dust. Good scents. He caught a gray-haired robust woman giving him the once-over from behind the gleaming counter of the front desk. Chances were good that she was Mrs. Pendleton, who hadn't been as easy to win over, he guessed, as Amy had counted on.

It took him only a second to orient himself. He found the mystery suspense section. The library was small, but they had a good selection. This is what he'd been missing, and better memories rolled through his mind. Memories of taking a rainy Saturday going from one bookstore to another, drinking espresso and browsing through the bays. Finding just the right story to read next.

He pulled out a favorite author's older book and read the dust jacket.

It was as if an angel touched him on the shoulder, stirring him from the book and leading him to her. Amy. He knew, as she glanced up from thumbing through a card-catalogue drawer, that some things happen for a reason.

Not that he was willing to admit his life was governed by more than fate. But it sure felt that way, and the shifting of his soul was as if a part of him leaned toward the light, toward life. Her.

Her hair was down, that's what was different about her. When she worked, it was always tied stringently back. Golden streaks rippled like water in her darker blond hair, buoyant and rich and so lustrous. Those golden locks framed her soft oval face, emphasizing the delicate cut of her high cheekbones and the fine curve of her chin. Soft rosy cheeks and a rosebud mouth, she appeared so fresh and wholesome, she was beautiful all the way through. He knew that because he could feel her spirit, which was all spring light. His heart thumped as if it was doing more than pumping his blood.

He was coming back to life. Amy was doing this to him.

What should have been painful was not. His chest warmed as if he'd downed a big mug of steaming hot chocolate, melting through him until he was no longer cold.

Across the way, she hadn't noticed him. Her slim fingers walked along the old catalogue cards. A wrinkle dug between her eyes as she concentrated. It was a cute thing, the way she bit her bottom lip and folded back a shock of hair that tumbled into her eyes.

She moved her lips, as if repeating a Dewey decimal call number, trying to memorize it. Then she shoved the tiny drawer shut and took off in the opposite direction, walking quick and sure, on a mission.

His soul ached when she disappeared into the stacks.

Brought back to reality, he realized he was standing in the middle of the aisle with a book held open in his hands. Shutting it, he clasped it by his side and followed her.

There was no denying what he felt. No denying that what felt like an elastic cord stretched between her spirit and his. He'd felt this before, but not this strong. Not so incredibly intense.

She reappeared, carrying a thin book, and that's when she saw him. Recognition brightened her features and her smile moved through him like spring wind through new leaves. Shaken, he gripped the solid wooden side of the book bay, but it didn't save him. He was falling, not physically, but in another way. His heart was tumbling, his senses spinning, his soul quieting until there was only her.

"Hey, I'm glad you showed up," she whispered, coming closer, the pad of her sneakers rasping loudly in comparison to the absolute stillness in the library. As if uncomfortable, she glanced around, folded a lock of hair behind her ears, and didn't meet his gaze. "Mrs. Pendleton is making up a card for you, on my account. Make sure you remember to get it."

"Are you on your way out?"

"Yep. I'm going to sit in the shade and read until school lets out. My errands have taken about six times longer than I thought they would."

"You have somewhere to go?"

"Home to clean my house. Now that Paige is back, I can get to the things I got behind on."

"I noticed your house was a complete mess. Terrible." It had been perfect, comfortable, tidy and homey. With just the right amount of chaos, like the toys on the floor, to make a person want to sit down on that deep-cushioned couch and stay forever.

Maybe it wasn't the comfortable living room that made him feel that way. Maybe it was Amy.

"I see you've found a book. Excellent. I guess I'll see you tomorrow morning. I'm working the breakfast shift. It's Jodi's day off." She took a step back, maybe needing distance, maybe wondering why he was staring at her without saying a word.

He knew why she was edging away, talking about work and acting as though nothing had changed between them.

Everything had.

"I'm done looking. I'll head out with you."

"Oh, sure thing."

He couldn't tell if it was surprise or fear that had her retreating.

As they walked together to the front counter, a calm sense of rightness breezed through him. It was as if that calmness took root and spread. It was odd, this link he felt with Amy. They moved in synchrony. He'd bet they were breathing with the same rhythm. Their hearts pumped at the same pace.

He had no business doing this, walking beside her as if he'd be there for the rest of forever. Waiting while she added the book to a small stack on the counter and glided it across the sparkling clean countertop to the librarian. He watched her bend to dig through her purse.

She produced the small laminated card and snapped it on top of the books. "Mrs. Pendleton, this is the man I was telling you about. Heath Murdock."

"Hello, ma'am."

The middle-aged woman peered over the tops of her glasses to give him a surly once-over and frowned as if he fell short of her standards. "I've got the card made up. Let me get it." Tight-lipped, she turned to sort through a small stack of paperwork.

Amy's nearness danced along his awareness, filling his senses. The apple-sweet scent of her hair and skin. The curve of her jawline as she lifted a graceful arm to check her watch. The rhythm of her light breathing, timed with his. She was color in his world of darkness and shadow. He wanted her more than he had the words to say.

Or the right.

Chapter Twelve

The librarian returned, took his book with tight-lipped suspicion and scanned the book and card. He watched, not at all surprised that the system was still the stamped date on the pocket card instead of the efficient computerized system he'd known in Portland.

Listening to the thud of the stamp, the snap of the book closing and the hush of the dust jacket sliding across the counter took him back to his boyhood days of checking books out of the country library. Good memories.

"It's due back in two weeks." Mrs. Pendleton gave him a look that said she'd hunt him down if he dared to be late or mistreat her book.

Yeah, the librarian when he'd been a boy

was just as protective of her books. Not blaming her at all, and knowing she needed reassurance since he was a stranger, he managed his most doctorlike tone. "Yes, ma'am. I won't be late."

Her brow shot up, as if in surprise, as if he just might meet her approval. Then she dealt with Amy's stack of books. Two hardbacks on astronomy and an inspirational paperback.

"For your boy?" He nodded toward the science volumes.

"We had to special order them, you know, the interlibrary loan thing. He's had to wait forever—well, according to *him*—so this will be a great surprise for him."

"Has he always liked astronomy?"

"*Moon* was his first word."

Mrs. Pendleton finished with her work and presented Amy with the stack of books. "It was good seeing you again, Amy. You tell Westin I've ordered a brand-new book on quasars, like he was asking me about last month. It'll be a few weeks yet before it comes in, and I've got to catalogue it, but I'll save it for him. He'll be the first one to read it."

"Oh, thank you!" Amy tucked her library

card away in her purse, grabbed the books—
all perfectly ordinary things.

She was not ordinary. Not to him. Looking at her made his eyes burn, like someone
who'd lived too long in the dark. Walking beside her made him ache from the intensity of
being next to her.

He held the heavy glass door for her. With
a quick, "thanks!" she waltzed past him,
leaving him dizzy. He followed her out into
the afternoon where leaves whispered and
birds chirped. Perfect clouds sailed across a
sky that was as blue as a dream.

Amy checked her watch again. "I'm going
to wait here until school gets out. No sense in
going home only to turn right back around."

"Doesn't he take the school bus?"

"We live too close, and he's only in kinder-
garten." She tucked that strand of hair behind
her ear again. "I suppose you're heading back
to the apartment?"

"Hadn't really figured on what I'd do next.
Maybe I'll just sit here with you for awhile.
It's been years since I've had the time and
the inclination to sit in the shade and read a
good book."

"There are some benches over there, beneath the maples. That's where I was going to wait. I can see the front doors of the school from there."

"Sounds good."

Amy chose the wooden bench that gave her the best view across the street and sank against the hard wooden back. It felt good to sit, she'd been on her feet all day, even if she hadn't put in a full shift at the diner. She'd worked the last three weeks almost straight through, sometimes a fourteen-hour shift. So she didn't feel a bit guilty thinking of all the things she still had left to do.

She let the sweet wind sweep over her and tangle her hair. Let the warmth of the afternoon soak through her. "It just feels good to relax for a minute."

"I don't suppose single moms get a lot of relaxation time."

"No." She laughed at the idea of lounging around in her robe and slippers. "Everything would fall down around my ears if I did that."

He took the end of the same bench and set his book next to him on the long length of boards between them. He stretched out his legs, drawing the denim fabric tight around his muscular legs. "It must be a lot to shoulder alone. A child, a home and a business."

"I don't mind. Besides, I'm not alone. I've got my sisters, and boy, do I owe them. There hasn't been a day that has gone by since Westin was born that Paige or Rachel weren't doing something to help out. Paige doesn't have a lot of spare time since she has a teenage boy and handles most of the business end of the diner. Yet she still finds time for me."

"She seems the type."

"Ben, that's our brother, he's half a world away in the Middle East. He's in the air force. And as busy as he is being an airman, he sends a monthly package of stuff for Westin, just to help out. I can't tell you how blessed I am."

Of course, she realized, it might not seem that way to him. She lived humbly, stretched every penny to make ends meet and sometimes she couldn't. Her car wasn't new, her house wasn't fancy, and her clothes were department-store discount.

But across the street in the third classroom down, where bright cutout flowers decorated the big windows, her son sat in the second row, fourth desk over. He was safe and happy and loved, with an extended family who cherished him.

Heath cleared his throat, his gaze following hers. "You seem pretty lucky to me."

His infinite sadness filled her. Tears burned in her eyes. "I learned long ago, the hard way, that I already had everything that mattered."

"The hard way?"

Oh, she didn't want to tell him. Nobody knew, although she suspected Paige had an idea, and Amy didn't want the clear respect in his gaze to dim or fade away. He'd see her differently. But she felt compelled, as if it was inevitable that she would tell him her secrets, the way he'd done his best to tell her his.

She took a shaky breath to fortify herself. To take time to find the right words. "I wasn't always the squeaky-clean Christian you probably think I am. It's not that I never lost my faith, I just took it for granted. Like living here in this small town where everybody knows everything about you because they remember when you were born and watched you grow up. I know you come from a big city, so this place must seem lackluster to you."

"No, I wouldn't say that. It must be tough, on one hand, because I'm guessing Westin's father is around here somewhere. Is he not involved?"

"Oh, no. When things got…complicated, Westin's father told me that he didn't want any entanglements tying him down—and if I thought he was going to be committed to anyone or anything, then I was wrong. He packed my bags and put me outside in the middle of a Seattle rainstorm. In November. Without the money from the paycheck I'd just cashed."

He remained silent, but she knew this story of hers wasn't what he'd expected it to be.

"I was just eighteen and I thought I knew it all. I left this place I thought was small and boring and dumb. I didn't even wait to graduate from high school, I wanted out of here so badly. Paige did her best, but—"

"Paige?"

She sensed his unspoken question. *Why not your parents?* "Dad died when I was seven in a hunting accident. Mom died two years later from lung cancer. She was a heavy smoker. So, Paige was sixteen and the state said she could keep us. She left school to run the diner. She got her GED but it was hard for her, handling so much responsibility, and I didn't make it any easier."

"I have a hard time picturing you as a rebellious teenager or living in a big city."

"The Lord looked over me or else I never would have made it. There were times when I was broke. I'd saved up my tip money from the diner for two years, and I had twelve hundred bucks in the bank. I thought it was a fortune. It went like water downhill. My car died halfway across the state, in a mountain pass, and the tow bill alone took a quarter of my cash."

"Not good."

"No. By the time I'd found a room to rent in a house in Seattle and paid first, last and the deposit, I was broke. But, like I said, I wasn't alone. A great job came my way. I started out bussing for a really nice waterfront restaurant. It was beautiful along the water. Seattle is so green, and the water is brilliant on sunny days and a soothing gray on rainy ones."

She closed her eyes, trying not to remember. Wishing more than anything she could go back and change her decisions. "Westin's father was the bartender at the restaurant. He was charming and about five years older, oh, I thought he was so smart and suave. Distinguished. I'd never had a drop of alcohol before I met him. I'd never done a lot of things. I was young and naive and I thought it was sophisticated to drink and go to parties, and when he asked me to live with him, I thought he loved me."

"You were in love with him." It wasn't a question but a statement, as if he understood.

Ashamed, that's all she felt now, but yes, she'd been so deeply in love. "I was just some innocent romantic girl who wanted to be loved when all he wanted was a maid and someone in his bed. Someone to borrow money from. I knew it was wrong, but I justified it. I wanted so badly for someone to love me, to really love me. And I just…compromised everything I believed in. Six months later I was pregnant, penniless and fired from my job for fraternizing. The restaurant, come to find out, had a strict policy against their employees dating."

"Was Westin born here?"

"No. I found a job in a diner, not in the good part of town, but the finer restaurants where the tips were good didn't want a pregnant teenage waitress, for some reason." She shrugged, trying to hide her pain.

There was no way she could hide anything from him. Heath breached the distance between them by laying a hand against her nape. The instant his skin contacted hers, a jolt of emotion so strong and pure rolled through him, from her heart and into his. A wave so dark with regret and hopelessness that his soul beat with recognition. She'd run from home looking for love and she'd found pain and betrayal.

In her heart she believed she was unlovable. That if she loved like that again, so wholly and true, it would never be returned.

He could picture how hard she worked, hounded and broken, spending long hours on her feet and her back screaming with pain as the months passed. He knew without asking she worked until she went into labor. And was back at work shortly thereafter. Exhausted, afraid, alone. Scared.

She saw that he understood all that she didn't tell him. It was odd, how they could speak without words. How he could know.

She sighed, a painful sound. "I came home two weeks later. I'd called Paige to ask if she could wire me the bus fare. She took me and Westin in and never said a word. She never scolded. She never made one mention of all the times she'd told me this could happen. She just...loved me. Like a big sister should."

Heath didn't say anything, so she kept talking. "That's why I'm here. I look around at the town I thought was so lame and boring, and I see people I've known since I was little. Friends and relatives and neighbors who say hi to one another and who pitch in if there's trouble.

"Did you know Mr. Brisbane and his morning group started a donation jar to help with the cost of the windows? It's not the benefit of the money, it's the thought behind it. I want to raise my son in this community of good people, well, mostly good people. I know how lucky I am."

She studied the elementary school again, growing quiet.

Yeah, Heath thought. In his opinion she *was* pretty lucky. "You put the battery in your smoke detector, like I asked?"

"As soon as I walked through the door."

"Good."

Was it his imagination, or was she leaning into his touch? She seemed to be, her skin warm and smooth, pressing toward him. He dared to come a few inches closer. Then it was as if nothing separated them, not distance or pain from the past. Not the fact that he had no future and that she didn't believe a man would love her enough to stay.

He only knew that he wanted to try. And he couldn't. "As you probably guessed, my wife and son died in a house fire. When our house caught fire, it was because of a short in the wiring. I had a late-night call—I used to work in an emergency room."

"Like a doctor?"

"Yeah. I was a doctor." He shut off the memories forcing their way up, memories that would break him all over again. He couldn't let them run wild, he could only take out one and leave all the rest buried.

Not easy, but he tried to find words for the past he'd never told another living soul. "There was a bad accident, a drunk driver took out a car full of high-school kids coming back from a football game. They were good kids, driving responsibly according to witnesses, no alcohol. The driver did everything he could to avoid the pickup coming at him, but there wasn't much he could have done."

"Did they all die?"

"No. Two kids died on impact, but three others were so critical the medevac didn't think one of them would make it alive to the landing pad.

"I worked nonstop in the OR. A whole team of us, I was working on just one kid. I got a letter from her mother, the day I walked off the job. Her name was Kari, I don't know why I remember that after all this time, but she'd been accepted to one of the Ivy League colleges on full scholarship. She had so much promise. I didn't know that when I was working on her, I just saw someone who needed me. I didn't think she'd make it.

"I tell you, I'd never been so exhausted, but we got her stable enough, closed, and got her into recovery. She did time in ICU, but she recovered. Instead of going home, I went in to assist another surgeon. It didn't make any difference, we lost the young man, and I was heading home, just coming out the ER entrance to go to my car when the ambulance pulled up. And my son—" His voice broke.

"My son." He couldn't say any more and put his face in his hands. "He was on the gurney and I—"

He shook his head. There was nothing more to say.

What could a person do to ease so much suffering? Amy felt helpless. This big powerful man so mighty and strong felt so fragile. Not weak, no, never that. But he'd been broken.

She laid her hand on the vulnerable nape of his neck, where his sun-browned skin was hot. Comfort. It was all she could offer him.

It was a while before he straightened, all the color drained from his face. He took her hand from the back of his neck and she thought, here it comes, he was going to push her away. It was what she expected.

But then he lifted her knuckles to his lips and kissed each finger. Warm and sweet and reverent.

"Christian was eighteen months, three weeks and five days old. The coroner said my son never suffered. The door to his room was left open, so my wife could listen for him in case he needed her, and the smoke took him. But she…she tried to get through the flames to the baby."

He shook his head as if he didn't want to remember, as if it were impossible for him to say the words. With care, he kissed her hand one more time and, as if with regret, laid her hand on the bench, away from him…and stood.

He walked away, the invincible line of his shoulders defeated. Across the street, the traffic monitors wearing their bright orange vests came out with their cones and flags. Amy doubted that he even noticed, although he was facing them as they spread out at the intersections, setting up the safety cones and chatting as they worked. Alone, he stood feet apart and braced, arms behind him, his head bowed.

Amy knew there were no words that could comfort him. There was no comfort for such a loss. She could say she was sorry, but what good were those words? She wished she could hold him until his pain stopped. Find a way to heal the broken places in his soul.

Across the street, a bell jangled shrilly, announcing the schoolday's end. Within a few seconds the doors flew open, busses were puffing into place, and children's shouts of freedom filled the air. Kids with lunch pails, kids with art projects, kids streaming to the busses and others arrowing toward the intersections. The monitors stood at attention, ready to direct the inflow of cars hurrying to jockey for position along the front of the school.

Life, it was everywhere he looked. Heath squeezed his eyes shut, but the brilliant colors and images remained like a snapshot in his head. The shrill screams, the gleeful laughter, the shouts as boys called out to other boys and the giggle of girls reminded him that life went on, without him, but it went on just the same.

"Mom!" A little boy was hopping up and down at the corner across the street, a paper he held flapping in the breeze.

Heath recognized Amy's son, dressed neatly in a navy T-shirt that said Astronaut In Training in white letters beneath a print of a space shuttle orbiting earth. The boy was so animated, leaping in place, hair sticking straight up, and a smudge of what looked like paint on his cheek.

The traffic monitors stepped out to hold up

traffic, their bright flags snapping. Westin sort of skip-walked across the street, separated from the pack of kids, and dashed across the grass to his mother.

"Look what I made. And I didn't make one mistake! And I got in trouble." To his credit, the boy tried to look contrite.

"What did you do this time?" Amy sounded stern, but it was only an act.

Heath wasn't fooled as she knelt to draw her child into her arms, holding him close, keeping him safe. Studying his artwork of Jupiter with the big storm and narrow tiny rings. Amy remarked over his excellent painting skills and then got him to hand over the note from his teacher.

"I talked when it was quiet time. I know." Westin rolled his eyes. "But it's very, very hard to be quiet all the time."

"On your second-to-the-last day of school? We'll talk about this when we get home, young man. Why don't you go see what books I got for you. They're on the bench, go look." With a loving pat, she steered him in the direction of the bench.

Heath heard Westin's, "All right! Excellent!" and was surprised it wasn't agony to watch the boy drop to his knees and flip open the first book. He was instantly absorbed by the color photographs from the Hubbell telescope.

Watching him, Heath felt his throat ache, trying not to look back into the past. Fighting to stay in the moment instead of being pulled backward into suffocating sorrow.

As if she knew how hard he was struggling, she came up beside him and laid her hand on his forearm. A simple gesture, but the connection reminded him that, for this moment anyhow, he wasn't alone.

This was a pretty fine moment in the right-here-and-now.

"Mr. Murdock!" It was Westin, holding open the book with care. "Mom! You gotta see this. Look at this cool picture. It's seventeen light years away. That's really, really far."

It hurt to look. It would have hurt more not to. Heath fought the tiny flicker of fondness for Amy's son. A little boy so different than his Christian would have been, but the boy made him remember the cheerful toddler babbling away, building his simple vocabulary of "Da!" And "No!" And "Uh-oh!"

"...Will ya, Mr. Murdock?"

Heath focused, realizing Amy's son was asking him something. "Sure." Whatever it was, he didn't mind. He just needed to think about something other than Christian. "What do you need?"

"Ice cream, but Mom's bringin' it."

"Sorry." Amy shrugged. "Don't worry about bringing anything. Just come as you are. With the upset over the vandalism, we didn't get to the welcome-home dinner we planned for Paige. And then we've got Westin's upcoming graduation to celebrate."

"I'm gonna be a first-grader!"

Amy saw the hesitation pass across Heath's face. It was strange how she could read his emotions. She knew he was uncertain about what he'd agreed to. She knew so many things that lived in his tattered heart. Those were the things that mattered. One day, he'd be gone, he was not a man to come to love or lean on.

But she loved him all the same. For the way he smiled, as if he wasn't breaking apart or remembering another little boy, while he hunkered down on the bench. "A first-grader, huh? That's pretty fine."

"Yeah. I know." Simply, Westin held out

the book and turned the picture. "Cool. Did you wanna see?"

Heath's eyes looked so bleak. Then he smiled, just a little, but it was like the full moon rising on a bleak night.

It changed everything.

Chapter Thirteen

Amy lit a second citronella candle, shook out the match and set it into the cooling barbecue coals. Supper had been simple grilled burgers over hot coals in the barbecue pit at her development's riverside park. Not fancy, but then, she figured Heath hadn't been living with luxuries since he'd walked away from his job as a surgeon.

After everyone had stuffed themselves with more dessert than was wise, it was hard not to drift off for a quick nap. The sun hazed through the cottonwoods and glinted on the swift river, moving faster for the snowmelt still occurring in the mountains.

The only one who seemed as if he wasn't

content was Heath, finishing off a second slice of lemon pudding cake. Paige's teenaged son, the one with the endless appetite, was working on his fourth piece of cake.

"See what you get to look forward to." Tender, Paige ruffled her son's hair on her way from the table. "Feeding a bottomless pit. I think the government ought to give two deductions for teenaged boys, since they eat enough for at least three people. Maybe even four."

"It makes sense to me," Rachel commented from the folding camping chair where she was watching over Westin and one of the neighbor girls who were wading along the river's tamer edge. "I'll start a petition. I'm sure there are a lot of people who'd sign it."

"Mom, is there any more cake left?" Alex set down his fork, his plate clean of even the tiniest crumb. "I'm still hungry."

"See what I mean?" Paige dumped the empties in the nearby garbage can and carried the cake plate over to him. "You might as well just eat all of it. Unless anyone else wants a piece. Speak up now or forever hold your peace."

She waggled the plate in Heath's direction, but he shook his head. He'd spent the entire meal being polite, speaking rarely and watching them just as he was doing now, his face set, his arms folded over his chest, so invincible and stoic it was hard to read his emotions. The shadows in his eyes remained.

Every time he noticed Westin, did he remember all that he'd lost? It troubled her deeply, how silent Heath was. She longed to comfort him. To lay her hand on his cheek and feel the pain of his heart move through hers. If only she could let him know he had a friend.

She held the last can up to him, dripping from the melting ice in the cooler. "More soda?"

"Nope. I'm good."

"There's one of Rachel's oatmeal cookies left."

"No thanks." He turned so he couldn't see the sun-warmed river where Westin waded, busily searching for rocks. He focused his interest on the last bites of cake on his plate, when really it was her he was trying to avoid seeing.

He'd tried to stay numb, tried to keep enough distance, but she pulled at him like temptation, making him want what was forbidden. What he could never let himself have again.

"Westin! Not so deep." She called out while she returned the can to the cooler and began stacking in the jars of mayonnaise, mustard and ketchup. "You know to stay where it's shallow."

"I know, but it's not high over here!" He shouted, hardly audible over the rushing gurgles of the river and the faster rumble of the white rapids farther downstream. The hem of his denim shorts had dipped into the water, growing darker and tugging down around his knees. "I gotta look for moon rocks."

"Look for moon rocks closer to the beach." She snapped a lid on the plastic container of macaroni salad. "I mean it, young man. Do it now, or get out."

"Okay, okay!" Westin took one more step. "One more moon rock. Please, Mom? Ple-e—ease?"

"No, you're out too far." Riverbeds were in constant change, and what had been safe only a few days ago might not be today. Amy didn't like how close her little guy was to the swift current that made no noise as it rushed endlessly downstream. "Come in a few—"

"Mommm—!" Westin's shout was cut as he plunged downward as if someone had grabbed his ankles and wrenched.

Amy watched in horror as he disappeared completely from her sight. He didn't pop back up again. The plastic lid slid from her fingertips and rolled out of sight. She couldn't believe what she'd just seen—he was gone. Completely gone.

"No!" She was running, twisting and turning her ankles as she hit the big river rocks along the outer bank. Three minutes. That's all she could remember from her safety days when she took swimming lessons. That's all the time she had to get into the river, find him and get him breathing again.

Panic made it seem as if she flew across the sandy shore and there was no pain as she hit a small boulder with the inside of her foot and dropped to her knees on ragged rocks. She surged upward, seeing only the spot where Westin had disappeared. The quick menacing waters rippled and rushed, as if he'd never been.

She heard splashing sounds and suddenly

there was Heath, running and then jumping as the water swallowed his feet and calves. Knee-deep he lunged, swimming like an expert, swift strokes that took him in seconds to where Westin had gone down.

Rocks impeded her as she hurried, lunging into the deep water, which ran across her skin like cold ice. With a power of its own, the river grabbed her and drew her away from where Heath took a great gulp of air, dove head first, his long muscled legs kicking water everywhere. And then he, too, was gone from her sight.

Please, God, please. Give me back my Westin. Oh, God, please. She wasn't the best swimmer and the current had her, she was spinning along like a big piece of driftwood past the point where Heath had dived. Heath surfaced in front of her, his big solid body a barrier that kept her from being carried away on the current.

Water sluiced off him. His skin was as cold as hers as he pulled her the few feet out of the strongest part of the current. "My cell phone's on the table. Someone call 911."

Heath took another great gulp of air, his black hair slicked to his scalp, his features sharp, his concentration focused. In a flash she could see the doctor in him, how he'd fought for his patients on the operating-room table. This is how he fought for Westin now.

As hard as she would fight. She dove again, seeing nothing but silt-tinted water and jagged rocks on the riverbed. She heard more splashing as Paige and Rachel joined the search. Shouting his name over and over as water closed over Amy's head and became silence.

How many seconds had gone by? She let the current take her as she desperately scanned from left to right. He had to be here. Her lungs burned and she came up, panting and coughing.

She could see Heath's dark form rising up to the surface, bursting through like a whale, spewing water. Empty-handed. No Westin.

Amy dove back into the water. She was going to find him. She was going to haul him up by his collar, lecture him on the dangers of getting into the deep current and he'd be grounded. For about six million years. He'd be grounded so good, he wouldn't be able to leave for college until he was forty-six years old. Like a mad woman, she let the water take her, keeping her eyes open as she tried to study the rock bed through the shifting green waters for the bright white T-shirt her little boy had been wearing.

"Amy!" A steeled hand gripped her upper arm, hauling her up. Her lungs exploded and she gratefully dragged in air.

Heath. He looked like a different man, harsh jaw set, eyes narrowed. He looked warrior-fierce. Marine tough. "He would have gone with the current. You get the others to start combing downstream. I'm going to go into the deeper part of the river. We don't have much time. Do you understand?"

She nodded, barely responding. Wild-eyed, she searched the silent water. "He's here. He's got to be right here."

"He isn't. The current has taken him." Heath couldn't tell her it was hopeless. He knew. A parent never gave up. A parent never stopped loving. A child was the sweetest gift of them all, the greatest blessing that God could give two people in love, and he'd been at work, saving other people's children when his had needed him.

He gave Amy, so fragile and valiant, a gentle shove into the calmer shallows where the others were combing the hip-deep waters. For a body. He couldn't tell that to Amy, as he filled his lungs with air and submerged.

Heath let the current take him, knocking him along the rocky bottom. Boulders bashed into him and he scraped over them fighting to see through the silt stirring up from the bottom. Westin couldn't have broken away from the powerful sweep of water.

It would have taken him from where the shallow shelf suddenly ended toward the middle, faster part of the river. It was like a jet stream, moving faster than the water surrounding it, and it would have taken him—

Darkness rose quickly ahead of him and the brutal force of the current slammed him against a submerged tree. Pain exploded in his left shoulder, he felt his fourth and fifth ribs crack and knew what the sharp arrow of pain was even before he felt the blood and the rest of the air in his left lung sluicing out of him. He had to get out of the water or he'd drown. He had a punctured lung.

Help me, Father. He prayed with all his might, to the bottom of his soul. He hadn't been able to save his son, who'd been dead on arrival, but he had to do this. His life was forfeit anyway. But Westin. *Please, let me do this one thing. This one right to put against the wrongs of my past. Please, do not let me fail.*

That's when he saw the flash of white. He clawed his way through the spear-sharp limbs, broken and bare, and prayed for one last ounce of strength.

"Over here!" Paige was waving the ambulance to the edge of the parking lot. Amy surfaced, hopes falling. The vehicle bounced over the curb and ambled across the grass, dodging picnic tables and barbecue pits and hauled up near the edge of the bank. Medics hopped out, and headed toward the river. Behind them a fire truck charged down the street.

No Westin. Time was running out. Treading water, losing hope, Amy started to pray one more time—

And then she saw Heath breaking the surface, Westin wrapped across his chest, and there was blood staining the river and streaming across Westin's torn shirt. Agony tore from her throat as she took out after them.

Heath was coughing. It was his blood.

Trickling across his bottom lip. His face was gray, and his gaze locked on hers and she saw deep inside him, his soul that was no longer breaking. He began to sink, and she was there, holding him up as the first EMT reached them.

"Hold 'em steady!" the young man ordered and started mouth-to-mouth on Westin.

His lips were still pink, his little face nicked and gashed. The medic breathed life into him and after three breaths, he moaned, moved and threw up the water he'd swallowed. Somehow they were at the shore; she realized her sisters were pulling them in. And they weren't alone.

Dozens of people had come out of their homes with blankets and pillows and first-aid kits, many more were in the water. They'd started a human-chain search. The cheers that lifted above the wind and the sirens and the fear brought tears to her eyes and gratitude to her soul.

The EMTs took Westin and he was awake, searching for her in the crowd. "Mama," he said, the same way when he'd been much littler and sick or frightened.

"It's okay, baby," she said as someone

wrapped her in a blanket and a fireman tried to take her vitals. "I'm fine. I have to see him."

She pushed her way through the big bulky men with medical gear and stood at Westin's feet, where he could see her while he was given oxygen and a heart monitor was set up.

"What about Heath?" she asked Paige, who'd come over to wrap her in a sisterly hug.

Rachel came with the news. They were calling in the medevac. "They're not sure he'll make it to the hospital, but they're gonna try to save him. And how I hope God is with him, for the difference he's made for us today."

"We're ready to go, ma'am," one of the EMTs told her.

Westin looked so tiny and helpless, his eyes searching hers for comfort. She'd been given back her son, and for that she would be thankful until her last day. But her thoughts were with Heath who lay motionless, as if already gone, surrounded by a dozen firemen and a score of strangers.

She had time for a quick prayer, hoping it

was in God's plan to save him, before she was whisked away, holding Westin's hand. And if not, then God's will would be done, but it saddened her. No, it went deeper than sorrow. Deeper than grief.

Please, Lord, don't let it end this way.

As they raced into the sunset, toward the hospital in Bozeman, she gave thanks for the sweet blessings in her life. And she knew beyond all doubt that she would be forever grateful to the loner who'd drifted into their lives.

Chapter Fourteen

Three days later

"Are you sure there's no one to come get you?" asked a concerned gray-haired lady wearing a volunteer's badge and exuding authority. "I don't think they let someone on pain medication just go home alone. I need to call someone about this."

"I didn't take my pain meds. And I'm not driving." He planned on calling a cab, but he didn't see the need to tell her that. He was alive, not that he was exactly happy about it.

When he'd felt his strength leaving him in the river, with Westin on his chest, he'd been glad he'd held out long enough to get the boy to his mom. Then he'd been relieved because it was over, finally, this struggle to live when he'd died long ago. The life drained out of him and he'd welcomed it. He'd yearned to see the bright light where he hoped his loved ones were waiting.

But he'd lost consciousness. When he'd come to in recovery, he knew God had failed him again. Failed him. Heath was alive. He'd come close to death, as he had so many times in the last few years. Every time God had snatched him back, had forced him into exile here, where Heath could not live, could not feel, could not love.

What kind of God was that?

Heath was done with God, done with faith, done believing there was any rhyme or reason or benevolent Father looking over His children.

He just wanted to get his stuff, get in his truck and leave. He didn't want to talk to anybody, he didn't want to see anybody, and since he'd asked and been told that Westin was just fine, there was nothing left to do.

No, that wasn't true. He had to say goodbye to Amy. And then he'd leave.

* * *

"When's Heath getting outta the hospital?" Mr. Brisbane asked as Amy freshened his coffee.

"As far as anyone could find out, maybe today, probably tomorrow." Amy tried not to let her disappointment show. Heath had made it through surgery and, while in recovery, had left orders that he didn't want to talk to anyone. Not even her.

The only reason she knew anything at all was that one of her favorite customers, who'd been her mom's good friend all those years ago, volunteered at the hospital in Bozeman and rooted out the information for her. Otherwise, Heath had not only written her off, but had also refused every gift, flower, balloon and phone call she'd tried to send, as well as gifts everyone she knew of had tried to send.

Paige was cooking this morning, her hair tied back, her face tight in concentration as she worked. Too tight. Amy knew full good and well that her sister was listening through the hand-off window. Paige, while she was grateful that Heath had saved Westin, was highly insulted by his self-imposed isolation.

"It just don't sound right," Mr. Winkler commented as Amy turned the pot to his cup. "I say something's wrong with that young man. It ain't good manners to go refusing folks who just want to say thanks."

"Ain't that the truth," Mr. Redmond added, holding out his cup for the next refill.

What they didn't know about Heath Murdock. Amy finished her rounds with the coffeepot and was saved by the order-up bell. She gladly fetched the order of ranchero chicken omelet, the daily special, piled high with hash browns and sausage links.

Frank seemed glad to see her. "That sure looks good. Say, you might want to let Paige know the Hayman brothers have agreed to pay for the damage they caused. You let her know there'll be a lawyer calling her later today."

"She'll be glad to hear it." The plywood still covered the first two windowpanes, but John had promised the glass, which had to be special-ordered, wouldn't take more than a few weeks to come in. "How about you? You aren't in uniform. Must be your day off."

"Yep. Thought I'd go fishing."

Things seemed back to normal. Westin had

graduated, and she was so proud of him. He was a big first-grader. Her baby was growing up. It made her glad and sad at the same time.

Someone called her name. Her cousins had gathered for breakfast in the back corner booth, and Karen was waving her over. She had a few minutes, so she stopped to chat. Karen's baby was smiling so sweetly, and Kendra was without her little girls today, for they were home with Grandma. Kirby, also sans her little ones, and Michelle, with her little Brittany snoozing in her car carrier tucked neatly into the corner, sat opposite them.

They were talking about T-ball practice, which was to start on Monday, and Karen offered to be the first car-pool driver, offering to ferry Westin, too.

A big extended family was a wonderful thing. She sneaked them free cinnamon rolls and lattes, and as the bell on the front door jangled to announce a new customer, she grabbed a trio of menus to seat the elderly Montgomery sisters. Through the window, as she was leading them to their preferred patio seating near the rose trellis, she caught sight

of a yellow taxi—all the way from Bozeman—slowing down at the front curb.

Heath. She knew it was him even before
she saw the silhouette through the windows
in the back seat. She recognized the mighty
line of that neck, the chiseled profile and the
dark shock of hair. As she waited for the
Montgomery sisters to slide into their favorite booth, she tried to look through the open
doorway, but the wall blocked her view.

Although she could not see him she knew
he'd climbed from the cab and was circling
the building. Still, after all they'd been
through, even after he'd cut off contact with
her, her soul moved in cadence with his.

The Montgomery sisters were finally settled and she laid out their menus and left, realizing only as she was already halfway
down the aisle that she hadn't filled their coffee cups…and she had the coffeepot in her
hand. She plopped it on the counter, rounded
the corner and headed straight out the back
door.

"Amy, don't be foolish—" Paige started
to say.

She slammed the door on her way out, to
cut her off. Foolish? No, she wasn't going to

make a fool of herself. Paige didn't need to worry. She marched up the stairs and beat on the aluminum screen door frame, staring through the mesh to the darkness within.

He couldn't have gone far. He'd probably beaten her up here by a matter of seconds. "Heath! Don't you hide in there."

"I'm moving kind of slow." There he was, ambling into sight from the back of the apartment.

Dear heavens, did he look bad! He was drained of color and thin, as if he'd lost weight. Several days' growth stubbled his jaw. He moved carefully, in obvious pain. Her anger ebbed like a tide washing out to sea as she saw how deliberately he kept his injured side still. The slow steps he took. The way he winced, as if in great pain he wouldn't admit to, when he opened the screen door and gave it a push.

She came in, but not any farther than just inside the threshold.

He'd brought his bag out. That's why he'd taken longer to let her in. He had the big battered duffel nearly full, the steel teeth of the zipper gaping like a great white shark's jaws. He added wrinkled clothes that must have been sitting in the dryer for a few days. He tossed in a toothbrush and a half-rolled-up tube of toothpaste.

"You came up here for a reason." He didn't sound angry but he didn't sound anything close to being glad to see her. "I heard Westin's doing good."

"They kept him overnight for observation but let him go early so he could finish his last day of school."

"Good for him." He turned his back, all steel and distance. He left no doubt as he zipped the bag closed. "This is goodbye."

"I know." She'd known this moment would come. It had been inevitable. How could anyone heal from wounds that went so deep? From losses that could never be made right? "I'm glad I got to know you, Heath Murdock."

"Likewise." He winced as he lifted the pack onto his good shoulder, took a couple of small steps forward, and wished. Man, did he wish. "I don't think I'll ever forget you, Amy McKaslin."

"I'll think of you every time I look at my son. He's alive because of you. There is nothing on this earth that I can do to match what you've given me."

"You've already done it." It was a hard thing to explain and he knew he'd fail at it, so he didn't even try. "Walk me out to my truck?"

"Okay." She held the screen door open for him and led the way down the narrow stairs with the same grace she'd always shown.

He'd been rude to her, refusing to see her in the hospital, and look at her, the woman who couldn't chase away a robin was the same one who offered him understanding that was unexpected and impossible.

"Maybe I should carry your bag, since you injured yourself pretty good rescuing my son."

"I'll carry it, thanks."

They walked the rest of the way to his truck in silence. The pleasant summer morning seemed the same as any other. Sprinklers ticking and clicking, mist spraying and the dog barking down the alley.

Heath waited until he'd stowed his bag before he turned to her. "Everything inside me is yelling at me to get going. I've got to. Do you understand? It's not about you."

"I know. You've been honest all along, and

I appreciate that. You're a fine man and it's been my privilege to know you."

Words escaped him, and he could only stare as the wind played with the fine wisps of gold escaping from her ponytail. She looked so beautiful, from the inside out, it made him awaken. The ice within him was cracking apart and the tundra of his spirit could not stand the change. He wanted to return to the blessed icy winter and hibernate forever.

But the heat of the day warmed him through. The flickering leaves, the shade from the trees and the scents of rose gardens and mown lawns and mist from the sprinklers made him long for blessings he could never have. Not ever again.

Still, the world teased him. There were the customers' cheerful voices rising and falling from the opened windows. The drone of a private plane soared overhead, and from somewhere far down the alley came the irritated cry of a toddler in one of the little homes as a young mother's voice crooned, "Did you fall down? Come here my sweet boy."

Life, it was everywhere. He couldn't escape it. He was breaking apart from the inside out all over again. He knew it was wrong but he took the step into thin air, knowing full well he was already falling to an inevitable doom. In truth he could not stand here pretending he could walk away from Amy and not feel a thing.

Because he couldn't. His heart was cracking into smaller pieces, surprising him that there was enough of it left to do so. He'd give anything to be able to stay and step into Amy's life like a man who hadn't failed everyone he held dear.

"I'm not going to try to talk you into staying. I know this is what you have to do."

"It is. I don't belong here with you." *Although I wish I did.* He fought the urge to pull her into his arms. To hold her, protect her and cherish her for all the days of his life.

If only he could deserve her. To have a life with her and her son.

She gestured toward the diner. "At least go get your paycheck. Paige is stuck behind the grill, and I know she wants to say goodbye."

He followed her, taking in the airy way she moved in her faded denim Levi's. He memorized the golden ripple of her hair in the wind and the sweet apple scent of her skin and the way her mouth looked even softer whenever she met his gaze. Memories were all he was going to have of her.

Until he stepped through the front door and saw the usual morning crowd. The retired ranchers and the commuters in their power suits, young mothers and the women whose children were grown. Families and single people in for a quick bite. Friends and neighbors and people who mattered to him.

Frank was the first to stand. Then the morning retirees. Heath watched, disbelieving, as person after person stood and began to applaud until the little diner was ringing with the sound.

Paige came out from behind the grill to thank him for Westin, for what he'd done for her family and pressed the paycheck envelope in his hand. He'd done what any one of them would have tried to do, and many had brazened into the river. He hadn't been alone in that water. He saw now he hadn't been alone when he'd pulled Westin to the surface.

Maybe, even, before that, when he'd lost

all hope. When the waters had been too murky to find his way.

"Come back real soon, now, you hear?" Bob Brisbane clasped him on the shoulder.

"That's right, we don't want you traveling too far." It was Clyde Winkler. "The diner hasn't had such a good cook in a long while."

"He's a doctor," Mr. Redmond corrected him. "He's not really a cook."

Everyone in the diner came to shake his hand, to wish him well, to express surprise and dismay that he wasn't staying.

Amy had disappeared by the time he was done. Paige was back behind the grill. New customers began to stream in, and so he took his leave. As he was walking away and starting his truck, he wondered what he was going to do now.

Faith was a funny thing. He'd thought he'd lost it forever, but it wasn't true. God hadn't left him, God hadn't given up on him. Heath didn't know why things worked the way they did. He only knew that he was standing at a fork in the road. That everything he'd lost— family, friends and a home—had been waiting for him here, in this small Montana town, all along.

He turned the ignition and put the truck in gear, taking his time and looking around. Amy was nowhere in sight, but he could feel her as if she were half of his soul. He didn't want to leave. She'd given him no reason to stay—if he could have.

It was with regret he put the pickup in gear and headed for the interstate.

Amy sat in the warm still air of the apartment because she couldn't face anyone and there was nowhere else to go, unless she wanted to leave the diner for some privacy. Plus, it gave her a perfect view of Heath as he drove away.

She watched his truck amble along the main street through town, slow in obedience to the posted speed limit. The vehicle grew smaller until the angle of the buildings hid him from her sight. Forever. That was all she would ever see of Heath Murdock, capable cook and, for lack of a better word, soul mate.

She ran her fingertips across the library book he'd left clearly in the middle of the coffee table. Sorrow drained all the light from her spirit, and she felt as heavy as lead.

The punch of pain in her chest wasn't her heart shattering. It couldn't be. She wouldn't let it be.

She didn't want the warm syrupy rich flow of affection to fill her up, but it did. She knew that loving Heath Murdock was the second biggest mistake of her life. Why was it the bitter truth that as responsible and hard-working and good a man that Heath was, he couldn't promise her anything more than Westin's father had? For different reasons, sure, but it was a pattern with her. One she'd been smart enough to escape this time.

This time she'd kept her dignity. This time she'd spotted danger before she lost her heart.

But it was no consolation as sadness overwhelmed her and tears started to fall.

Chapter Fifteen

Good old Oregon rain. It fell in a misty drizzle that was so fine, it seemed to hang in the air. Heath had forgotten what a vibrant green Portland could be in early summer. The cemetery seemed to shine with greenness. The deep velvet green of the grass, the dark forest-green of the cedar and fir trees. The brighter newer greens of the aspens and maples.

Three years today Heath traced his finger along the date etched in the marble. His wife and son shared a grave. He knew that's what she would have wanted. His dear wife and son. He wished he could go back in time and find time for the small things, to check the batteries in the smoke alarm so he could be now where he belonged, with his family. That's what he'd wanted, all this time he'd been grieving. He wished he'd perished with them.

He didn't know why he was here to lay white roses on one grave and tie floating balloons to the other marker. But somehow it was part of God's plan. He was no longer bitter or despondent. Because he had something he thought he'd lost with his grief.

Good memories. Of a happy marriage. How they'd anticipated Christian's birth, how happy they'd been the day he'd come home. How one little boy who had brought so much chaos had also brought love and joy.

His cell phone jingled, and he reached into his coat pocket and checked the caller ID. Good, he'd been expecting this call. Heath answered, heard the good news and stood in the rain. He just breathed in the fragrant grass and trees, heard the sound of car tires on wet pavement on the busy road at the side of the cemetery.

He'd spent a few weeks handling things that should have been taken care of long ago.

But he was done. He'd put his affairs in order and he was free.

Free to go home.

The pad of a footstep had him turning around. His mother had flown up from Kansas, and she stood beneath the wide brim of an umbrella, her eyes gleaming with emotions only he could understand.

"Have you forgiven yourself, finally?" she asked, loving. Always loving.

He nodded. Somehow things had changed. And he knew why. God had led him to Amy. God had given him a second chance.

Maybe. He was ready to find out. He took his mom by the hand and escorted her through the rain and grass.

"Westin?"

The house was unusually quiet. Amy dropped the armload of staticky, dryer-fresh clothes on the couch cushion. The hum of the pedestal fan in the living room breezing cool wind across her face was the same, but there was something different in the air. She couldn't place it until she stepped into the kitchen.

It was the scent of roses. She could only think of one person who would bring her roses—Heath. There, on the pink Formica table lay a dozen pink roses, perfect petals cupped tight, as if they were getting ready to open. Her favorite kind, too, and there was no way he could know it. She caressed the silken buds and turned toward the sound of her son's voice outside, blowing in with the wind.

"Wow, I hit it! I really did!"

Was he out there with Westin? Then she heard Heath's rumbling baritone, warm with a chuckle. "You sure did. That was some hit. Do you think the neighbor lady will let us go into her yard to get your ball?"

Heath. Her heart wrenched seeing him for real standing in her yard, illuminated by the bold bright sunlight. He was unaware she was at the window, and his back was to her as he approached the chain-link fence. He looked fine in his usual jeans and T-shirt and with a baseball cap shading his eyes.

"Westin, is this your baseball?" Mrs. Nash's jagged voice, made shaky by the first stages of Parkinson's, was more beautiful for her kindness.

Amy could see her sidling up to the fence, holding a small white ball in the palm of her hand. The wind shifted, carrying away the strands of the conversation, but she was spellbound watching as Heath took the ball, smiled at Mrs. Nash, and then turned with the ball in hand, held the way a pitcher did, ready to throw.

"I'm ready! I'm ready!" Westin ran backward and held up something bulky in his hand—a new baseball mitt.

Heath sent the baseball sailing in a slow arc across the front of the lawn. Westin, instinctively keeping his eye on the ball, wove back and forth and then stepped back, holding the stiff glove up and the ball plopped right in.

"All right!" Westin turned toward the window, and then grinned when he spotted her behind the screen. "Did you see, Mom? Did you see?"

"I saw. That was excellent, baby."

"I know!" Pleased with himself, he reminded her so much of her brother, a natural athlete and naturally confident.

What was Heath doing here? He probably had no idea what he was doing to her. What she'd been trying to deny ever since he'd walked into her life that stormy night. The gentle scent of tea roses filled her kitchen and brought tears to her eyes, because she didn't know how she was going to hold onto her heart now that he'd come back.

"Mom! Mom!" Westin pounded up to the door and used both hands to shade his eyes so he could see her through the mesh screen. He was out of breath, wheezing a little, but his face was rosy from playing and, she hoped, happiness. "Me and Mr. Murdock are so thirsty, we're gonna dry up like this. Whoosh!" He flickered his fingers, as if what he was saying was perfectly clear.

"Well, I certainly don't want you and Mr. Murdock to go whoosh."

"Like dried-up dirt!" As if he were choking, Westin made a fake gagging sound, because he was in such a good mood and he knew it would make her laugh.

Careful to keep her eyes averted, she retreated to the fridge and pulled out two cans of black cherry soda and a pitcher of sun tea. "Can you take a glass of ice tea out for Mr. Murdock?"

"It's Heath." There he was, on the step behind Westin, shading his eyes, too, with both hands. Oh, he looked good. With the sun burnishing him, he looked younger, bolder. Brighter. "I'm a great fan of black cherry cola."

"Mom! Me and Mr. Murdock, we're alike! We both like baseball and we both drink cherry pop! And look! Look what he got me. It's a real baseball glove, for T-ball! And I can catch real good with it! You saw, right?"

"I saw."

Heath stood in the background, hands fisted at his hips, so invincible and stoic it was hard to read his emotions. She needed to be realistic. He'd probably come back just to say hello, like so many of the customers in the diner had asked him to. That was all. It would be smart to hold back her heart.

But she feared it was too late. "Westin, did you say thank-you for the glove?"

"Yeah! Ooh, thanks for the pop!" He loped away, feet pounding, confident that she'd come to watch.

She pushed the screen door open. Heath hadn't moved; he was standing on the cement walkway that cut through the middle of her lawn. Petunias brushed his shoes in bright, splashing colors and it was strange to have him here, in the middle of her yard, when she'd tried so hard to banish him from her thoughts. From her dreams.

She gripped the iron railing and she didn't remember the stairs or her feet padding on the concrete. Only that she came to a stop in front of him. He towered over her, blocking the sun and, standing in his shadow, she could no longer deny the truth in her heart. He was the one. The one who would be her one true love. Forever.

And he wasn't hers to keep.

"Thank you for the lovely flowers."

"And you look even lovelier." He laid his hand against her face, cradling her tenderly.

She pressed into his touch as the shine of his soul moved through hers. There was no more darkness or grief. Only hope.

He'd faced his past. She could feel it. He could go back to his old life, or maybe a new one somewhere else, a dedicated surgeon and such a very good man. He deserved all the happiness he could find.

It took all her dignity to keep her voice steady and her hopes from crashing to the ground. "It's almost lunchtime. Why don't you stay for the meal, as our treasured friend of the family?"

"You're fooling yourself, if you think the reason I'm standing here is friendship. I don't want to be your friend."

Her bottom lip trembled.

Yeah, he knew what she was feeling. He felt the same. As if he was taking a step off the northern rim of the Grand Canyon and looking at the distant rocky floor beneath him. And stepping into thin air, anyway, knowing he was going to fall. But he had faith.

"I've come for you and your son." Tender love rose through him until he was so full he could hardly speak. But he'd gone through a lot to get to this point in his life, and he was going to do this right. "I know you've been hurt before, and you don't want to trust any man like that again. But, Amy, you are the blessing I thought I'd never find. If you agree to be my wife, I vow to cherish you above all others. If you marry me, I will never hurt you, never betray you, never leave you."

This couldn't be happening. Surely this was a dream. She had to be hallucinating or something, but Heath's hand against her cheek trembled, and she could feel his genuine love for her, soul-deep and everlasting.

It was the same love she had for him in her soul. "You came back here to propose to me?"

"Not empty-handed." He pulled a ring from his pocket. A rich gold band with a big center-cut stone. Brilliant and perfect and probably expensive. "Amy, will you do me the honor of becoming my wife? To honor and cherish for the rest of my life?"

"Oh, yes!" Tears burned in her eyes as she leaped up to hug him, holding him tight. So very tight. Joy lifted her up as Heath wrapped his arms around her and lifted her off the step and kissed her long and sweet.

Her soul sighed, complete.

As he slipped the ring on her finger, she could see a glimpse of their future. Of happy days just like this with the breeze whispering through the trees and the sun smiling down on them together. As a happy family.

As she followed her son up the front steps, she remembered to give thanks for this unexpected blessing. The sweetest of them all. Heath took her hand, kissed her cheek and they went into the house together.

* * * * *

*Coming in September 2005
from Love Inspired, watch for
Jillian Hart's next installment of
THE McKASLIN CLAN!
Ben McKaslin returns home a hero,
but can the wounded military man
be healed by love?
Find out in* Heaven's Touch....

Dear Reader,

Thank you for choosing *Sweet Blessings*. It was such a joy to return to THE MCKASLIN CLAN. Cousin Amy, the youngest of her family, is a single mom who works hard to provide for her small son. She's given up on believing that there are men who are noble, strong and faithful in this world. Until Heath Murdock wanders into her family's café for a late-night meal. She recognizes in him a great wound. With God's help, both Amy and Heath discover that true love can heal even the greatest sorrow.

Wishing you the sweetest of blessings,

Jillian Hart

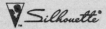